Cookie Cutters & Sled Runners

Cookie Cutters & Sled Runners

Natalie Rompella

ISBN 978-1-338-34922-1

12 11 10 9 8 7 6 5 4 3 2 1   18 19 20 21 22 23

Printed in the U.S.A.   40

First Scholastic printing, December 2018

Cover design by Sammy Yuen
Cover illustration by Simini Blocker

To my fourth grade teacher, Mrs. Jaronik.

Cookie Cutters & Sled Runners

Chapter 1

It was the last day of summer: the last full day Lily and I could spend together creating new recipes before middle school got in the way.

Popcorn Cake . . . Purple Raspberry Pudding . . . Brownies with a Gummy-Bear Glaze . . . I flipped to an empty page in my recipe binder and added our latest creation: Sprinkle-Cake Cookies.

"Mmmm, these are delish!" Lily gushed, tasting one before they even cooled. "Ana, you *have* to try one." She slid a cookie onto a plate for me.

After washing my hands, I grabbed a fork and knife and sat down. I cut off a small piece and slid it carefully into my mouth, as if it were something fancy, delicate, and French.

"Well, what do you think?" Lily asked.

I smiled and nodded. Soft like cake, but still chewy like a cookie. The sprinkles—Lily's idea—added a nice crunch and made the cookies look festive.

"These are really good," I said. "And just what our cookbook needs. Maybe we can add a chapter called 'Colorful Creations.'"

"Totally," she said, closing her binder and smiling. "So . . . cookies are done. Ready to look at our schedules?"

Lily had gotten back from summer camp late the night before, and even though we were both dying to know what classes we had, we'd promised to wait until we were together to open the schedules the school had sent us. But when she had gotten to my house, I couldn't bring myself to look. We had to make some comfort food first.

I got us each two more cookies, and we sat at the kitchen table.

"On the count of three, let's open them," Lily said.

I gulped. No more stalling.

"One, two, three!"

As I carefully slid my finger under the flap of my envelope, Lily ripped into hers.

Before I could even pull out my schedule, she started jumping up and down like a game-show contestant. "I got Ms. Meyer for first period!"

Everybody knew Ms. Meyer was the best teacher at Jefferson. Not only was she super nice, but she let her students drink flavored water in class and made hot chocolate for them in the winter.

I slid my schedule out of its envelope. *Please, please be the same as Lily's!*

HOMEROOM/PERIOD 1: ENGLISH . . . My gaze slid across the paper. MR. CREED.

Who?

"Never heard of him," Lily said, reading over my shoulder. "Guy teachers are usually really cool and funny, though." She took a bite of her cookie and added, "And maybe he'll be cute." I made a face, and she shrugged. "Let's see what classes we have together."

She had science when I had math, math when I had PE, PE when I had science . . .

"Seriously?" Lily said. "Well, at least we have lunch together, right?"

"Yeah," I said, trying to keep my voice from quivering, "but we'll be separated for *all* of our classes." What could be worse than middle school without Lily? We had been in the same class since second grade.

Neither of us knew what to say, so we sat in silence for a minute, gloomily eating our cookies.

Then Lily got up and poured herself more milk. "These cookies are good, but they make me thirsty. Maybe we can add to the recipe, 'Serve with a tall glass of milk.' What do you think?"

I blinked at her. That was it? She was already over it?

I looked down at my lap. With my thumb, I began writing A's on the palm of my other hand to calm my nerves. How could I possibly go into sixth grade alone? What if I never even found any of my classrooms? Or I got lost in the hall where the eighth graders were? *A, A, A.*

And then there were the problems I worried about every year: What if I noticed my chair had dirt on it? Or the teacher wanted to shake my hand? What if I needed to wash my hands, but the bathroom was super far away?

If Lily and I were in classes together, she could block me while I wiped off my chair or distract the class as I sanitized my pencil. But she wouldn't be there.

I drew more A's. It was an old habit: A's for my name when I got nervous. Which I was.

Germs freaked me out. Thinking about them always made me wash my hands. A lot. And it got worse when I was stressed or nervous about something—like starting middle school and finding out I'd pretty much be doing it without my best friend. My only friend. "It's okay, Ana," Lily said. She put her arm around me, careful not to touch me with her cookie-crumbed fingers. "I can walk you to your first class if you want. It'll be okay."

I just hoped she was right.

ANA MORGAN AND LILY CRAWFORD'S SOON-TO-BE-FAMOUS SPRINKLE-CAKE COOKIES

1 box yellow cake mix

2 eggs (wash shells beforehand)

$\frac{1}{3}$ cup oil

$1\frac{1}{2}$–4 tbsp water

2 tbsp rainbow sprinkles (using tweezers, pick out the red ones and throw them out)

1. Wash your hands with antibacterial soap. Sanitize all baking surfaces.
2. Preheat oven to 350° F.
3. Pour cake mix into a large, clean bowl.
4. Add eggs and oil to the bowl. Stir until blended.
5. Mix in just enough water so that the batter sticks together. Add sprinkles until the mix looks colorful.
6. Spoon tbsp amounts of dough onto an ungreased baking sheet. Bake for 9–11 minutes or until the edges are slightly golden.
7. Using a clean potholder, remove the cookie sheet from the oven. Place cookies on a rack and let cool.

Chapter 2

After Lily biked home, I added a couple of my own flourishes to our recipe in my binder. You can never use the words "wash," "clean," or "sanitize" too many times in a recipe.

Lily and I had been cooking together since the summer before second grade, when we'd met in Little Miss Cookie Camp. Right after meeting, we'd invented Apple-Pie Cookies together—we'd even sprinkled cheddar cheese on top, like they do in New England. Our counselor couldn't believe that two seven-year-olds came up with the recipe, but we really did. And that had just been the start of our cooking careers.

Since then, we had invented over fifty recipes, all completely original and almost all delicious. We planned to use them for our sixth-grade Explorations Project—the only thing I was still looking forward to about school.

Explorations was kind of like a science fair, but you could do any kind of project you wanted to, like research a famous person or create a robot.

Our cookbook—and samples of our creations, of course— would definitely be everyone's favorite project. Not only were our recipes yummy, but we had cool chapter titles like Noisy Snacks, Triangle Treats, and Skewered Specialties. We'd been planning our project for over a year.

As I closed my binder and caught sight of my school schedule on the table next to me, I sighed.

I unfolded the schedule to look at it again, hoping I'd misread it the first forty-three times. Nope—same classes. Same problem.

I looked around the kitchen. Mom and Dad would freak when they came in. But not because I had baked—they actually liked my creations. It was the cleanup that bothered them.

That day I'd used two types of disinfecting counter spray, about a quarter of a roll of paper towels, and four dishrags. I knew that when Dad came home and saw all the cleaning supplies out, he'd want to see my hands. The previous November, I had been so worried about a math test in school, my hands ended up so chapped and dry from washing them so much, he banned me from baking for a week. With middle school starting soon, my hands were once again on their way to Chapped City.

A few years before, Mom and Dad had made me see Dr. Taylor about my freaking-out/washing bonanzas, aka obsessive-compulsive disorder, or OCD for short. She had me do all sorts of stuff, like touch the floor with my bare hands without washing them afterward. She said that if I could handle super-extremely-gross things like that, I wouldn't flip out with a hand-washing marathon after doing normal things like turning a doorknob.

I had gotten way better, but I knew I'd always have to push myself not to imagine twenty million *what-ifs* (as in, *What if a germ speck lands on my hand when I'm washing them in a public bathroom and multiplies, causing me to die a long and painful death?*)

Leaving my schedule on the table, I put the cleaners in the cabinet, shoved all the paper towels into the garbage with my foot, and hid the dishrags in the hamper. There—evidence gone.

I grabbed some grapes and went up to my room.

The minute I walked in I saw my guinea pig, Bernie Toast, sniff the air to see what I had with me.

I had gotten Bernie at an Adopt-a-Pet day at the local pet store three years ago. Mom and I had gone there to buy a goldfish—an animal that was constantly soaking in water seemed like the perfect germ-free pet—but the minute I saw Bernie Toast, I fell in love.

He'd been sitting there, a nameless guinea pig with wiry, pitch-black fur. He'd looked kind of like a big scouring pad with eyes. And he'd been staring at me, waiting for a home.

At that moment, all my thoughts of washing and germs had disappeared.

And even though I often washed my hands at the *thought* of someone sneezing, holding Bernie had never seemed to bother me one bit. Lily was the only one who understood that.

"Maybe you're immune to his germs, kind of like a coat of armor," she had said when she first met him.

It made total sense: Bernie was my safety shield against all my worries.

"Hey, Bernie," I said, putting a grape into his cage and saving a few for myself. "Middle school starts tomorrow."

He blinked.

"What if my OCD makes me do something weird, like wash all my pencils in the bathroom? People will totally make fun of me." I popped a grape into my mouth. "And Lily's not in any of my classes, except lunch." I sighed and sat down on my bed. "I don't know what to do."

Bernie nibbled away on his grape, like he was giving it some thought. I did the same.

Bernie couldn't keep me safe from my worries at school. And now, Lily couldn't either. What was I going to do?

Chapter 3

The next morning, I got up before the alarm even went off.

I had laid out clothes the night before. Usually I had plenty of time in the morning, but sometimes my OCD got in the way, so I had wanted to be prepared. I smoothed out my plain blue T-shirt on my bed. I hoped that was the sort of thing other people would be wearing, too—or at least that I could just blend in wearing it. I slowly got dressed.

After I pulled my hair back into a ponytail, I gulped and said, "Bernie, today's the big day."

He grunted as if to say, "No worries."

I hoped he was right.

I packed up my lunch, a recipe I had come up with over the

summer: Back-to-School Pad-Thai Tuna Sandwich. Peanut butter and tuna made for a surprisingly delicious combination. Maybe this could be a good day after all.

But as I walked to the corner to meet Lily, all my panic returned. Even she seemed nervous, pulling on a blond, noodle-like curl and letting it spring back, again and again.

"I'm so nervous—but excited too, right?" she said.

"I guess," I answered.

After we walked in silence for a block, Lily got me talking about how to make our Sprinkle-Cake Cookies even better, and I began to relax.

But Jefferson Middle School was only five blocks from our block. We made it in less time than it took to scramble an egg.

Think about Bernie, I reminded myself. I pictured him looking up at me with his no-worries smile, and I was able to breathe naturally again. Until the first bell rang.

Everyone tried funneling through the doors at once. Just as I made it up to the entrance, someone gripped my arm with a slimy hand and cut in front of me, leaving a clammy cold spot where we'd touched. *Ewww.* Luckily I had my antibacterial hand sanitizer for these kinds of emergencies. I stopped to squirt some into my palm and rub it on my arm. But when I looked up, Lily had disappeared, swept away in the current of students.

"Lily!" I shouted.

"Ana! Find me at lunch!" she yelled back from somewhere in the crowd.

Finally, I saw her light curls springing up and down as she was pulled through the hallway.

After breaking free of the crowd, I trudged up the stairs to the second floor, looking at the map I had printed of the school and trying to remember where my first-period classroom was.

On the way, I passed a door with a sign that read WHAT'S COOKIN' IN MS. MEYER'S ROOM? and felt a pang of jealousy.

But maybe Mr. Creed would be into cooking, too. Maybe he was a former chef. A former *pastry* chef.

As I passed Ms. Meyer's classroom, I could see Lily inside already. She was deep in conversation with some girl who had a pink stripe in her hair. As I watched, they both laughed like they'd known each other for years.

I hadn't even found my classroom, and I'd already been replaced by a pink skunk.

Finally I reached Mr. Creed's room. The sign on the door said MR. CREED. ROOM 14. MIND YOUR MANNERS.

As I walked into the room and found a seat, I tried to tell myself to stay positive. Even if Lily wasn't in my class, there had to be other kids I knew from my elementary school in it, right?

Lily and I had been so close for so long, I hadn't ever needed to get to know the other girls from elementary school. And I guess part of me had always been afraid of what they'd think about my OCD.

But as others came in, I still hoped to see someone I knew—someone to at least say hi to.

No one.

I pushed a loose strand of hair behind my ears and smoothed out the back of my ponytail. All the other girls had fancy hairstyles—complicated braids or blond highlights. My hair was brown and straight and usually pulled out of the way so it wouldn't get dirty or fall into my food as I was making it. Lily once told me its color and silky texture reminded her of chocolate mousse. But she could make anything sound delicious.

The bell signaling the start of class rang, and a couple more kids flew through the door.

"I made it, Mr. Creed," shouted a boy with an earring. "I'm not late, right?"

That's when I noticed that the teacher was already in the front of the room. He had his back to us and was writing a list of *Do Not*'s on the chalkboard. He stopped writing DO NOT COUGH LOUDLY to say, "You are late. Rule number seven: Do not be tardy."

Mr. Creed wrote one more rule on the board, then turned to face us. We all stopped talking.

"Good morning," he said. "I am Mr. Creed."

Mr. Creed looked like a tall Munchkin from *The Wizard of Oz.* He had one of those curly mustaches, and the top of his head was bald. So much for Lily's theory that he'd be cute.

He walked between our desks with his hands behind his back, barely clasped together around his tomato-shaped body. "Just because you are sixth graders, and thus new to Jefferson Middle School, does not mean I will take pity on you. Now—"

Just then the classroom door creaked open, and we all turned to look. A girl wearing cargo pants, a thick hoodie with the words HUSKY POWERED on it, and furry brown boots walked in. A couple people snickered; everyone else had on shorts and sandals. She took her time closing the door as we all stared.

"I am so glad you decided to show up today," Mr. Creed said. "What is your name?"

"Dasher Hopkins," the girl said, her nervous smile revealing a mouth full of metal braces.

"*Dasher*?" Mr. Creed said.

"Like the reindeer?" a boy in the back row blurted. "Sweet!"

The class laughed until Mr. Creed cleared his throat.

"Well," she continued, "my name is actually *Dana*, but everyone calls me Dasher." She smiled again.

Mr. Creed picked up a clipboard on his desk. "Yes, Ms. Hopkins, you are in this class. And the roster lists you as Dana, so that is how I will refer to you."

There were more muffled laughs, and I sank lower in my seat, hoping Mr. Creed wouldn't find something I was doing wrong, too. I would die if my teacher yelled at me on the first day.

"You are late. Find a seat so I can continue."

"Oh, okay," Dasher said, looking around. There were three empty desks left, and two of them had other kids' stuff on them. The last was next to me. She slid into the chair.

I peered over at her. Her face was covered in freckles—like someone had sprinkled her with paprika—and she had long, messy, pecan-colored hair. She opened her notebook and began doodling as Mr. Creed kept writing rules: RULE NUMBER ELEVEN: DO NOT USE CONTRACTIONS IN MY CLASSROOM.

After getting our locker assignments, Mr. Creed had us take turns reading aloud from the school handbook. I glanced over at Dasher again. She appeared deep in thought . . . WITH HER PENCIL IN HER MOUTH. Yuck! Didn't she know anything about how communicable diseases spread?

Finally the bell rang.

"I expect that, by tomorrow, tardiness will not be an issue," Mr. Creed said. "You are dismissed."

As I walked out the door, I let out the breath I'd been holding.

But then I felt a hand on my arm and someone said, "Wait!"

I spun around to see Dasher standing there, her hand still on me. I smiled as if it didn't bother me, but she moved her hand away anyway.

"Did I miss anything when I was late?" she asked.

"I don't know, but I think everything's in the packet he gave us," I said, holding up the thick handout. Across the top, it read ENGLISH EXPECTATIONS.

"Gotcha. Thanks. Pretty intense teacher, if you ask me."

"Yeah. I—" I almost told her how nervous Mr. Creed made me. But what if she laughed at me? "Never mind."

She looked down at her schedule. "What period do you have lunch?"

"Fifth."

"Me too!" she squealed. "Maybe I'll see you then. Shoot— gym's on the other end of the school. Better go. See ya!" She sprinted off.

I looked down at my schedule: Math. Alone, of course. I trudged down the hall.

I could feel my shoulders relax for the first time all day when I spotted Lily waiting for me outside the cafeteria, fixing her makeup in her little powder mirror.

"Finally!" I said. "It felt like I'd never see you again!"

"I know. Crazy, huh? I am starving with a capital S," she said, putting her mirror in her purse. "Did you see what's for lunch? I didn't have time to make one."

"Seriously? Meat loaf?" I said when we got in the lunch line. If I were in charge of school lunches, I would've created a dish with a catchy name, like Have a 'Souper' First Day Back!, and served Lily's and my ¡Taco Soup! Instead, the meat glistening under the heat lamps smelled horrible. Even worse, it had a rusty tinge and a thick red glaze on top. Ketchup.

I shuddered. I hated red foods almost as much as I hated germs. What do ketchup, red jelly, and spaghetti sauce all resemble? Hint: it starts with b and ends with l-o-o-d.

Lily poked me. "You haven't listened to a word I've said, have you?"

"Sorry." I motioned to the hunks of meat. "I was distracted."

"Didn't you bring your lunch?" she asked.

"Yeah, but are *you* going to eat it?"

Lily sighed. "Fine, I won't get it. But only because it looks gross, anyway." She grabbed a tray and put a banana on it. "And you have to share some of your lunch."

"Deal."

We sat down at one of the long cafeteria tables. The floor was dusted with litter dropped by the lunchers before us: scraps of bread crusts, splotches of purple jelly, and even a Frisbee of bologna.

I sanitized my hands before pulling out my sandwich and handing half to Lily.

"Thanks," Lily said with a mouth full of banana. "Hey! There's Via. She's in my math class." She waved and called "Via!" as I turned to look.

It was the girl with pink hair. Who was now walking over.

"Hi, Lil," she said, dropping her tray on the table.

Meat loaf.

Lily motioned at me. "This is Ana."

I plastered a smile on my face.

"Can I sit here?" the girl—Via—asked, and she sat down without waiting for an answer. "I'm Via, BTW," she said to me as she opened her carton of milk.

"Love your nails. And your rings," Lily gushed. Via's short fingernails were painted lime green, and she had a ring on each finger.

"Thanks. Did you guys meet today?" she asked us.

"No, we've been best friends since second grade," I said, thinking Lily would pipe in. But she was too busy still admiring Via's rings.

"All my old friends went to Lincoln instead of Jefferson," Via said, like it was no big deal.

I would've freaked if Lily and I had to go to different schools.

"Wow, those are some major boots over there," Via said, pointing.

I looked up. "That's Dasher," I said. "She's in one of my classes."

"*Dasher*? Like the reindeer?" Via asked.

Dasher looked around the cafeteria for a long time, holding her lunch tray, before sitting down by herself at the end of a table.

"I think she just moved here from Alaska over the summer," I said. I had overheard her telling one of the girls that while we were putting our things in our lockers.

"She must not have known it'd be eighty degrees out here," Lily said.

"I could totally give her a fall makeover," Via said. "You know, plaid skirt, black army boots, faux glasses . . ." She began cutting into her soggy meat loaf with a spork. *Gross, gross, gross.* I put my back to her a little so I wouldn't gag.

"What? Do I have a something coming out of my nose?" She wiped at it with her hand.

"No, no. Ana just has issues with red foods," Lily said, like I was being rude.

I almost choked on my sandwich. I couldn't believe Lily would say that to a complete stranger. My red food thing was top secret. It's not like I could help it—it's part of my disorder.

"You have a problem with *red* foods?" Via asked.

"Yeah. Uh, I don't eat them."

"Even ketchup?" Via asked. "I looove ketchup!" To prove it, she stuck her finger in the meat loaf glaze and licked it off.

I turned even more and tried to picture something else. *Bernie Toast eating a piece of lettuce . . . A hot fudge sundae with black-licorice relish . . .*

"Well," Via began, "at least my lunch is better than what someone else is eating. It smells like a dead fish in here."

I spun around to face her. "It's a Pad-Thai Tuna Sandwich. I created it. And yes, it has albacore tuna in it."

"Whoops," Via said, giggling. "Sorry. My bad."

"Ana's really good at coming up with new recipes," Lily said.

"For people or cats?" Via joked. "Speaking of cats, I found the cutest leopard-print tights at the mall yesterday."

The rest of lunchtime, Lily and Via talked about fashion. I just nodded here and there as if I knew there was a difference between boyfriend-cut and slim-cut jeans. But I felt like I was in a fog—or invisible.

Finally, Via looked up at the clock. "'Bell's about to ring. I have to give Lauren-from-Español my number, since Señora Richards confiscated her phone during class." She got up. "See you in math tomorrow, Lily. Bye . . . what was your name again?"

"Ana," I said, a little too quietly.

"Wha?"

"Ana," Lily said as if she were my mother.

Via walked over to the garbage and tossed what remained of her hunk of bloody meat.

"Omigod. I can't believe you said that to Via about your sandwich," Lily said. "She's so nice."

"Nice? What were *you* thinking, telling her I don't eat red foods?"

"Jeez, Ana. I was just making conversation," Lily said. "It was more like telling her you don't like pickles or something. You know?"

"Whatever," I said and forced the zipper closed on my lunch bag.

I could only hope that Via would find someone else to sit with tomorrow. But she still had math with Lily. Would Lily tell her about my OCD? No, she'd never do that. We were best friends. Analily and Liliana. And we didn't need anybody else.

RECIPE FOR CLEAN HANDS

6–10 pumps liquid antibacterial soap, divided
towels—as many as needed (from linen closet)
1 bar soap (unopened)

1. Run water until it heats up. Wet your hands.
2. Squirt 1 to 2 pumps of liquid soap into your palm. Rub hands together vigorously. Let soap sit on hands for 30 seconds.
3. Rinse soap off under the hot water. Be sure to remove entire layer of soap, since any contaminants from your hands are now joined with the soap particles.
4. Dry hands with a towel. Use force, as friction can also kill germs.
5. Rinse bar soap under tap. Using the soap like a crayon, "color" over the top, sides, and palm of each hand, creating a thick layer of soap. Rinse and dry with a fresh towel.
6. Repeat steps 2 through 6 as many times as needed.

Chapter 4

"Mom, I'm home," I called out, making a beeline for the bathroom. I had barely kept it together at school, but once I got home, my brain exploded with germ overload.

Was my locker handle clean? What about the chairs? Did anyone cough near me?

Mom intercepted me in the hallway just outside the bathroom. "How was school?"

"Not good. Awful, actually. Isn't there any way to get me switched into Lily's classes? Even just one?"

She shook her head. "Sorry, Ana. We've been over this."

"But I have *OCD*. Doesn't that count for anything?" It had made a difference in the past. The year before I'd been allowed to take extra time on tests because my OCD liked to play with my brain when I was stressed about things like exams.

"This doesn't have to do with your OCD," Mom said. "And I don't think Dr. Taylor would approve of you switching classes just because you're not with your friend."

"Fine. Can I wash my hands now?"

"Speaking of your OCD, how did you handle it today?"

"It was the *first day*, Mom. So, about how you'd expect. Can I clean up now before I die of contamination?"

"Yes." She gave me a stern look. "But limit it to three minutes."

"Three and a half."

"Three." Mom finally released me. "Oh, before I forget: Grammy called right before you got home to see how your first day went."

That cheered me up a bit. Grammy lived five hours away in Michigan. She didn't have a cell phone, call waiting, voicemail, email, or even an answering machine, so hearing from her was always a surprise treat.

Grammy wasn't even my own grandmother—she was Lily's. I didn't have any grandparents still living. But Grammy always treated me as if I were one of her own grandchildren. And sometimes it even felt like I was her favorite.

After a scrub session worthy of a hospital staff, I went to my room to call Grammy. Bernie Toast peered up at me from his cage as I came in. I picked him up and gave him a gentle squeeze that made him squeak with joy. "Hey, Buddy. Did you miss me?"

With Bernie in my lap, I called Grammy and told her everything, including what happened with Via.

"Ack—I'm sure things will go better tomorrow," Grammy said. "Did you make any new friends?"

"No," I said. "But that's okay. Lily and I are still best friends."

"You can never have too many friends."

Even though Grammy couldn't see it, I shook my head. Lily and I didn't want any other friends. We were fine with it being just the two of us: Liliana and Analily.

"So, have you baked anything new lately?" Grammy asked. Lily and I went to visit Grammy every year, and we loved making up new recipes—most of them using cherries. Unlike other red foods, cherries reminded me of Grammy. And they were everywhere in Michigan in the summer.

I told her all about Lily and my new cookie recipe.

"Speaking of which," I said. "I need to go to Lily's to work on our Explorations project. We're going to see if we can use baby food in brownies instead of vegetable oil, like we've done with applesauce before."

"Wonderful. Save me a copy of your cookbook when it comes out."

"I will. Hugs," I said.

"Hugs, Ana."

When I walked into Lily's house, she was already in the kitchen laying out ingredients.

I opened up my binder to take notes on our process.

"Ms. Meyer is so cool," Lily said as she washed her hands for an extra long time for my sake. "I totally wish you were in her class with me."

"I know. Mr. Creed is scary."

"That's what Via said, too. She has him for social studies."

Via again.

"What'd you think of her?" Lily asked, spooning liquefied bananas into a bowl.

"Who? Via? She's okay, I guess." I added in the sugar.

"It turns out we have four classes together. Isn't that fab? And her name's really Olivia but she goes by Via. *So cool.* Did you know she's into fashion, like me? And she knows how to speak three languages, including Pig Latin; and she skateboards, knits, and—"

I stiffened up. "Does she cook?" *Please say no.*

"Not much. Just cookies with her mom and stuff, but she says she'd like to. I showed her my new Pork-and-Bean Dip recipe in English, and she said it sounded rockin'." Lily walked to the refrigerator and pulled out a carton of eggs.

I stirred the batter in silence but then couldn't take it anymore. "So do you still want to be partners for Explorations, or not?"

"What? Of course I do! I just told her about one of my recipes. No biggie. You and me have been planning Explorations for centuries. *You* still want to work with *me*, right?"

"Of course, Liliana."

"Fab, Analily. And once we finish our cookbook, I can send a copy to the cooking channel. They'll totally put us on their kids' baking show."

Unfortunately, this recipe was not going to make it into the cookbook. The brownies tasted okay, but the consistency was weird—kind of like baby food. Hmm . . . that wasn't a bad idea. I jotted it down in the "To Try" section of my binder: Baby's First Brownies. I bet no one had ever thought of that. What baby wouldn't love brownies?

Chapter 5

"Ta-da!" Lily said the next morning, handing over a small container. "They're Caramel-Apple Skins. And here's the recipe. I added a note about washing hands, just for you. And"—she held out a bag of white, skinless apple slices—"I thought Bernie might want the rejects."

"Aw, he'll love you!" I slipped the baggie into my backpack. Lily thought of everything—like she knew me as well as I knew myself. There was no way Via could come between us.

But when we headed for our lockers, I saw Via waiting right by Lily's.

"Lil!" she shouted. "Long time no see!"

The two of them grabbed their stuff, then linked arms and walked into Ms. Meyer's room.

Great.

As I walked down the hall to first period, I realized I had forgotten to leave my lunch bag in my locker. I was turning around to go back when—*Boom!*—I collided into a boy as big as a grizzly. All my belongings went flying in every possible direction.

"My stuff!"

The boy gave me a look like, "That stinks," and kept walking.

As I hurried to pick up my math book, someone walking by kicked it by mistake. It skidded across the floor like a hockey puck and flew right over the landing, making a smack sound as it hit the first floor. *No!* The bell was about to ring!

Deep breaths. Deep breaths.

"Here," someone said. I turned, and the first thing I saw was a pair of furry boots. Dasher handed me my pencil.

"My books—my lunch—my stuff's *all over the place!*" I cried out. "My math book. It's all the way on the first floor. Mr. Creed'll kill me if I'm late. And where's my assignment notebook?" I hugged the only book I was able to locate to my chest.

"I'll go get your math book," she said. "You find your assignment notebook. I'll meet you in class."

"Then you'll be late—"

"Hurry up and go," she said, "or we'll *both* be late."

I ran through the hallway until I found my assignment notebook; it was wedged under a classroom door like a doorstop.

I wiggled it loose, hurried to Mr. Creed's room, and sat down, trying to catch my breath. I quickly squirted some hand sanitizer on my assignment notebook and wiped it off with a tissue. Then I looked at the desk beside me. Dasher's chair was still empty.

The bell rang, and Mr. Creed closed the door.

No Dasher.

"Good morning, class," Mr. Creed began. I gulped.

"Good morning, Mr. Creed."

"Today—"

The door squeaked open, and I cringed. Dasher walked in, a pained smile on her face. "Sorry," she mouthed to Mr. Creed as she tiptoed toward her seat.

He pursed his lips. "I will see you after school, Ms. Hopkins."

Dasher nodded and put my math book and lunch bag on my desk before sitting down.

"Thanks," I whispered to her. "Sorry."

She smiled and waved her hand like a detention was no big deal.

"Now, where was I before I was so rudely interrupted?" Mr. Creed continued. "Ah, yes, Explorations."

Explorations! I opened my notebook to a clean page.

"As you may know, every year Jefferson partakes in an independent study project, otherwise known as an Exploration. It is a chance to pursue a course of study related to something of interest to you. You will have the option of studying a topic in detail in one of the following areas: the arts, the sciences, the social sciences, or mathematics." He paused after each topic to write its name on the board.

"This project will count toward your English grade, regardless of the subject area. Now, in the past—" He stopped to take a girl's ChapStick away as she was applying it. "I have seen projects that were disgraceful: 'Which nail polish lasts the longest' counting as a science fair project . . . a graphic novel listed in the arts and literature division . . ." He tossed the ChapStick into the trash can. "In my class, I will not tolerate such mediocrity."

I glanced over at Dasher, who didn't even seem to be paying attention. Instead, she was drawing some sort of map.

"Can I do my project on my stamp collection?" some clueless boy blurted out. "I've got over a hundred stamps."

"Mr. Evans, you are in violation of four of my rules, not including the use of a contraction. For that, I will see you after school. And no, your stamp collection will not be a good use of *my* time."

The boy sank down in his seat.

"An example of a stellar project from past years: one student determined whether chemically treated water had an effect on invertebrates such as daphnia. This project happens to have been my son's. But I am sure you can find a similarly appropriate topic."

He leaned on the front of a boy's desk, and the boy sat up straighter. "Now, this year I have changed my requirements for Explorations. You will all be working *in pairs*."

"But I'm—I am—doing a project by myself," the boy with the stamp collection said.

"No, you are not," Mr. Creed said. "No one from my English classes will be working as an individual this year."

A bunch of kids groaned. Others began shouting out to one another, trying to claim a partner. I didn't bother, since I already had Lily as a partner.

"Enough!" Mr. Creed interjected. "I have taken the liberty of choosing your partners for you. This will force you to come to an agreement on a project and work cooperatively, fairly, and respectfully with another pupil."

"But, Mr. Creed," a girl in the front row began, "I would like to work with my friend, Carrie. In another class. Sir."

"You will be working with a pupil *in this class*."

What? My heart began to race. A partner in this class meant . . . I wouldn't be able to work with Lily. But we had planned for this forever!

"Your partner has been randomly assigned to you from a list of your classmates. Listen for your name. If I hear so much as a whimper, you will be staying after school."

Mr. Creed walked over to his desk to get his clipboard. "Mr. Hoffman, you will be paired with Ms. Santiago."

The girl who must have been "Ms. Santiago" slapped her hand over her mouth to control her disappointed groan.

"Mr. Borne, you will be paired with Mr. Lewis."

On and on he went. As each person's name was read, I quickly scanned the room to figure out who matched it. I was relieved to see that both Mr. Evans—stamp collection boy—and the kid I'd been referring to in my head as Dirty-Fingernail Boy were both assigned to someone else.

"Ms. Morgan—"

I looked up from drawing a bazillion A's in my hand.

"You will be paired with Ms. Hopkins."

I could feel Dasher Hopkins smiling at me. But I didn't turn my head. Was I dreaming this? There was no way this was happening. Lily and I had to be partners. She was the only one who could do the cookbook with me. I bit my lip to keep from crying for the rest of class.

Dasher was probably nice and all, but Lily and I had planned to work together since *fourth grade*. I couldn't even imagine doing my project without her. How could I cook with a stranger? And Dasher wouldn't exactly win awards for cleanliness.

Finally, the bell rang.

I had planned on thanking Dasher for finding my math book and apologizing again for causing her to get a detention. But I was so upset about not being partners with Lily, I was afraid I'd start bawling in front of her if I spoke.

"Hey, Ana, you wanna meet—"

Acting like I didn't hear her, I bolted out the door.

Since my lunch bag had skidded across the floor, I didn't consider anything in it still edible, and I threw it out. As I met up with Lily in the lunch line, I silently prayed that the cafeteria would be serving something normal, like toast or soup.

Nope: ham. Another food that I was particular about—all those lines of white fat running through it, sometimes a dot of red here or there. I looked at the other lunch choice: spaghetti in a marinara sauce.

It wasn't a good day for me and the color red.

I bought a chocolate milk, and Lily and I went over to our table. Via was already sitting there. Ugh.

"Is that all you're having?" Via asked, looking at my lone carton of milk.

"I guess."

She opened her lunch bag and pulled out her sandwich. "Is it because of my comment yesterday? About your fishy dish? Do you wanna borrow money to buy a lunch?"

"No, that's okay. I don't really like ham or spaghetti."

"Here, then." Via tore off half of her sandwich. "You okay with PB&J?"

I hadn't had a peanut butter and grape jelly sandwich since I was about six years old. I stared at it. Via had used one regular piece of white bread and the heel of a wheat loaf to make it. Normally I wouldn't eat food from strangers, since you never know their prep routine. But I was super hungry, and she was trying to be nice. I nodded.

Via opened her lunch bag again and pulled out a second, smaller bag. "And my Nana made these cookies. They're rockin'."

"Thanks," I said, smiling as best I could after my horrible morning. Via and Lily both watched as I took a bite of the sandwich. Ugh. Via had also used *crunchy* peanut butter—about a whole jarful. I chewed and swallowed, chewed again, and drank half my milk to wash it down. "Mmmm," I said. "So good. Thanks."

Lily and Via went back to eating.

"So, did your English teacher pass out the stuff about Explorations?" Via asked, taking a cookie from the bag on the table.

I hadn't planned on upsetting Lily with my news at lunch, but I couldn't hold it in after Via asked.

"Um, Mr. Creed. He—he assigned partners."

"Yay! Finally!" Lily said, not understanding.

"No. I mean I have to be partners with someone in my English class."

"What? He can't do that, can he?" Lily asked, furrowing her eyebrows. "Make you partner with someone random?"

Via brushed cookie crumbs off the table with her hand. Yuck. "That's Mr. Creed for you. What a barrel o' fun."

"Who'd you get partnered with?" Lily asked me.

"The girl from Alaska. Dasher."

The three of us looked across the lunch room to where she was sitting alone. She was trying to cut her ham with her spork. Then she gave up and picked it up to eat with her hands.

Via looked back at me and raised her eyebrows. "Wow. That should be interesting."

"So you're sure we can't do our project together?" Lily whined.

I nodded, fighting tears.

"I'll work with you," Via said to Lily. "We'll do a really awesome project."

I gulped down a mouthful of sandwich without chewing and turned to look at Lily. She smiled at Via. Was she actually considering this?

Mr. Creed was ruining my life.

"Have you guys thought of what you're going to be for Halloween yet?" Via asked. "I am so excited for the dance!"

Another famous thing about Jefferson was the school's big Halloween dance. Everyone knew all the middle schoolers went to it instead of trick-or-treating every year. Lily and I had already started talking about costumes we could do together.

"I'm not sure," Lily said. "I did see some really cool jungle cat costumes at the mall, though."

Cat costumes? We had talked about being salt and pepper shakers. I drew A's into my hands under the table. *A, A, A . . .*

"Ana? Are you all right?" Lily asked.

"Yeah, you're, like, totally zoning out," Via said. "Why aren't you eating?"

I looked down at the sandwich. I had only taken three bites. "I'm pretty full."

"Already? No wonder you're a stick. At least try a cookie before I eat them all." She slid me the bag. "Keep 'em."

I looked at the two cookies in the bag and pictured Via's grandma mixing up the batter. What if she was a finger-licker?

"Lily made these apple skins that we ate earlier, and I'm still stuffed." I totally wasn't—my stomach had already digested the few bites of sandwich I had eaten and was ready for more. But I just couldn't do it. I zipped up the bag of cookies and patted it. "I'll save these for later."

"Whatevs." Via looked at the clock. "Wow, lunch sure flew by. Adios, ladies."

As she headed for the trash bins, Lily turned to me again. "You sure you're okay?"

What could I tell her without sounding like a jealous baby? That Via was ruining our friendship? Instead, I nodded like everything was fine.

"See you later, then."

I got up and tossed the sandwich and the cookie bag into the trash with all the rejected oink lunches. As I was sanitizing my hands on the way out the door, Via walked past.

"You're cleaning your hands again? You're, like, obsessed with washing them or something!" She giggled, then gasped. "Oh—there's Thomas Bradley. He's *so* crushing on me. I gotta hide." She hurried off.

Now, not only was I losing Lily, but I had Via teasing me for washing my hands too much.

I hated middle school.

Chapter 6

Squeak, squeak, squeak, Bernie called out to me from his cage on Saturday morning.

"Mr. Toast, are you hungry?" I asked, slipping some timothy hay through the bars of his cage. "After I make lunch, you'll get a taco, too, okay?" He seemed to nod as he chewed.

Whatever my family ate, I tried to give Bernie the fruit-or-veggie equivalent: raw pumpkin seeds if we had pumpkin bread, apple slices when I made apple-cinnamon pancakes. Today, he'd get lettuce from my Saturday Spaghetti Taco.

Just as I was grabbing my binder, the doorbell rang.

Maybe it was Lily saying she'd rather work alone on her Explorations project than work with Via. Not that that was likely.

I had to admit that Via was a more exciting partner than me. She dressed like she was going to a rock concert. Every day. She jingled when she walked, thanks to all the bracelets she wore. And she was allowed to watch R-rated movies.

If I were a food, I would be a piece of plain white bread, not even toasted. She would be a Belgian waffle with fruit, whipped cream, and a side of brown-sugar-glazed bacon.

"Ana," Mom called from outside my bedroom door.

"It's Lily, right?"

She poked her head in. "No, it's a girl from school. She said that the two of you are working on a project together?"

Dasher? I blinked. I didn't know what to say to her. That I was still trying to be partners with my friend?

"Um . . . I'll come down once I'm dressed."

I took my time before heading into the living room.

Dasher was standing there in a camouflage jacket, her hair in two braids. Next to her was a little boy wearing a matching jacket. And they were both chowing down on a snack Mom had set out for them on the dining room table.

"Hey," Dasher said like it was totally normal for her to stop by. "I got your address from the school directory. This is my brother, Cubby."

"I'm four till November," Cubby said, holding a scruffy-looking, gray stuffed bear. As I got closer, I realized it was probably a polar bear, and it was just extremely dirty.

"Do you like Noodles, my bear?" he asked, excitedly. He wiggled the bear around like it was dancing.

"He's very . . ." all that came to mind is *in need of a good washing*, but I finished with "furry."

"Dasher and Cubby just moved here from Alaska," Mom said like they were all old friends.

"My mom told me I could invite you over to work on our project," Dasher said. "Do you want to?"

"I—I can't," I said, stalling. I still needed time to figure out how to get out of working with her. "My parents need me to help them . . . dust today."

"Dust? When have you helped with that?" Mom said, ruining the plan. "You can go, Ana."

"Great!" Dasher said.

"Where do you live, Dasher?" Mom asked. Dasher's name sounded especially weird when Mom said it, like she was interviewing one of Santa's reindeer.

"On Old Hill Road."

"Oh, your family moved into where Leona's Pumpkin Farm used to be, right?" Mom asked.

"Yeah. Leona was our grandma."

"Leona was a lovely lady," Mom said. "We were sad to hear she passed away."

I nodded and put my head down. Every Halloween before this one, Lily and I had gotten our pumpkins at Leona's. Everyone did. Leona even let everyone pick out their pumpkins while they were still growing on the vine and scratch our names into them. Once it was pumpkin season, we would find our personalized pumpkin and take it home.

"Come on, let's go," Dasher said.

Mom gave me her *you-can-do-it* smile and practically pushed me out of the house. "Bye!"

Before I knew it, she shut the door.

"You have a bike, right?" Dasher asked, putting on a helmet covered in dog-paw stickers.

I nodded.

Dasher got on her bike, and Cubby jumped on behind her, putting his feet on the pegs of her back tire.

"What do people do for fun around here?" Dasher asked as we rode.

"Bake?" I said, but then realized that might not be something Dasher would do. "Skateboard? Go to the mall? Play basketball?" I didn't really know what other kids did.

"Basketball's cool, I guess."

"So what was Alaska like?" All I knew about the state was that it was really far away and sometimes had polar bears.

Dasher smiled. "Awesome. Colder than here—I keep forgetting not to wear a jacket when I leave the house. It was fifty degrees when we left."

"Had you been to Illinois before you moved here?" I asked.

"Nah. Washington is the only state in the lower forty-eight that we've been to."

"Lower forty-eight?"

"Yeah," Cubby said. "The other states besides Alaska and Hawaii. There are forty-eight other ones. My mom told me."

"I see," I said, smiling a little. He was kind of cute.

"How many states have you been to?" Dasher asked.

I shrugged. "I've never really kept track. Twelve?"

"Did you know there are alligators in Florida? And armadillos in Tesses?" Cubby asked.

"Texas," Dasher corrected him.

"That's what I said," Cubby whined.

Finally, Dasher and Cubby turned into Leona's dirt driveway. I rode slowly so I wouldn't get covered in the caramel-colored dust that caked Dasher's boots and bike tires.

The pumpkin patch was in pretty bad shape. There were only a couple of small orange balls poking out of the ground, and the vines were a big tangled mess.

"Yeah, Dad didn't get Grandma Leona's green thumb," Dasher joked.

As we approached the house, Cubby and then Dasher hopped off the bike. Dasher dumped her bike on its side, while I carefully flipped down my kickstand.

Leona's—now the Hopkinses'—house was smallish, and really old. It had a huge rusted tractor standing next to it like a sculpture. In the distance was an ancient barn instead of a garage. It was very different from my house, which was new and clean and looked like all the other houses in our neighborhood.

"Come on," Dasher said motioning for me to follow her in the side door.

"Ma, Ana's here!" Cubby yelled.

"Be right back," Dasher said, and she and Cubby went into the kitchen, leaving me standing in a hallway by myself.

The inside of their house still smelled like breakfast—eggs, overcooked bacon, and pancakes. A couple of family pictures hung on the walls near the coat rack. In most of them, that dirty polar bear was cradled in Cubby's arms like a fifth family member.

A woman came into the hallway, wiping her hands on a towel and walking toward me. "Well, hello, Ana. I'm Mrs. Hopkins." She grabbed my hand to shake it.

Oh no.

Hands were so dirty. One reason I didn't like meeting new people—adults, that is—was because they'd reach out their germy hands for a handshake. Shaking hands with people was part of my therapy, but I still didn't like it.

When she let go, I wiped my hand off on my pants as discreetly as I could.

"I'm gonna show her the dogs," Dasher said, walking out of the kitchen with a handful of pancakes.

I breathed a sigh of relief—Dasher liked animals, too. Maybe we had more in common than I thought. I hoped her dogs were little cute ones, like teacup poodles.

"All right," her mom said. "Did you want something to eat first, Ana?"

Dasher held out a limp pancake. "Yeah, you want one?"

"Oh, I'm fine," I answered, stepping back.

"'Kay. Then follow me." Dasher motioned us outside.

"Sorry, Noodles, you need to stay here," Cubby said.

Dasher rolled her eyes at me. "Mom, Cubby won't leave us alone."

"Cubby, you need to practice for your piano lesson on Monday," Mrs. Hopkins said.

"But I want to hang out with Ana and Dasher."

"Not today."

Cubby stomped away, and Dasher and I went back outside.

As we turned the corner to the backyard, my jaw dropped. Dasher didn't have a dog or two—she had a couple dozen. The first thing I saw was millions of homemade wooden doghouses. Some were triangular; others were square. And the dogs were separated into two large pens with chain-link fences, each dog attached to a tall metal pole by a chain.

As we walked closer, one dog barked, then another, then another, like a row of dominoes. They all started jumping up and down like pieces of popcorn in an old-fashioned popcorn popper.

"What is this—a dog farm?" I asked over the noise. The closer we got, the more it smelled like dog. I tried not to breathe in too much.

"Pipe down!" Dasher called out to them and then turned to me. "Not exactly. Guess again." Dasher opened one of the gates and went into the pen. A dog jumped up and licked her face. "Hey, Pickles."

I looked around. There were gray and white, black and white, brown and white, and even yellow and white dogs. Some looked liked wolves, with pointy ears and scary eyes.

"Do you guys breed dogs?" I asked, hoping that the dogs couldn't sense fear, break down the fence, and maul me.

"No," she answered and gave Pickles part of a pancake. "They're sled dogs."

"Sled dogs?" I pictured a cartoon dog wearing a ski hat and sledding down a hill.

"Dogs that are used for sled dog racing?" she said. "You've never watched a race?"

I backed away from a dog that was trying to sniff me through the fence. "No. We don't have anything like that in Illinois."

"So I've noticed. It's probably because it's like living in an oven here. Sled dog racing's pretty big back home. The dogs are totally bummed that we moved here."

"So why did you guys move?" It seemed like even the dogs didn't want to leave Alaska.

Dasher looked down. "My dad lost his job more than a year ago. When Grandma Leona died, she left us this house to do what we wanted with it. When Dad came out here for the funeral, he wound up finding a job finally. So we had to pack up and move. It sounded fun at the time, but it's very . . . different." She kicked at the dirt with her boot. "Anyway, we'll get used to it—even the dogs."

"So are these huskies?"

"Some. Alaskan huskies. And a couple—like that one—are Eurohounds. Our Eurohounds are a cross between a German Shorthaired Pointer and an Alaskan husky." She nodded at a short, skinny dog whose fur was spotted like a brown-and-white cow.

I looked around again at their backyard. There were dogs and fences as far as I could see. "Did your yard come like this?" My backyard had a flower garden, a decorative sundial, and a grill.

Dasher laughed. "I wish. When we moved here, me and my dad had to put up all these fences and spinners." She pointed to the poles the dogs were attached to. "And we had to make new doghouses and everything. We actually had all the dogs in our house for a week. It was crazy! They hated being cooped up inside."

I couldn't imagine a house filled with dogs. A single guinea pig was one thing. But tons of dogs didn't sound sanitary. I shook the thought out of my head. "So, when are we going to talk about our project?"

"We will." Dasher held open the door to one of the pens for me.

"Oh. I—I'm not going in there."

"Why not?" Dasher asked, petting one of the gray dogs as it licked her face. Yuck.

"Aren't they dirty?"

"Haven't you ever had a dog before?"

"No. I have a guinea pig. Bernie Toast."

"Dogs aren't any dirtier than guinea pigs. Especially mine. Wanna feed one a treat? They're all really friendly." Dasher handed me a pancake through the fence.

"Thanks, but—"

As I was handing it back to her, one of the beasts put its paws up on the fence, stuck its snout through, and grabbed the treat from my hand, leaving a trail of saliva across my palm. I shrieked. "He just got me all wet!"

"That's Luna. She loves treats."

"But she just got my hand all wet!"

Dasher looked at me funny.

"Sorry, I better get back home," I said in a panic. "I'll see you later." I turned and headed for my bike, holding my contaminated hand up in the air so it didn't touch my bike handle. I could feel the spit bubbles still on it.

"Wait! Ana! What about our project?" Dasher called after me. But I got on my bike and pedaled all the way home, the smell of saliva wafting up at me. What diseases could humans catch from dogs? I'd have to look it up.

Dasher was nothing like Lily. How could Mr. Creed have put me with her?

When I got home, I burst through the back door.

"Did something happen?" Mom asked, jumping up from the couch.

"Yeah, I got drooled on." I was still panting.

"Drooled on?"

"Dasher has dogs. Millions of them." I ran to the kitchen sink and told Mom about the sled dog stuff as I let the water run over my hand.

"That's neat that she likes animals like you do."

I squirted soap on my hands and lathered away. "Dogs are different than Bernie."

Mom cleared her throat. "How's your ERP coming?" ERP—exposure and response prevention therapy—was the therapy Dr. Taylor made me do for my OCD. It involved things like purposely shaking someone's hand, touching the floor, and only washing my hands for three minutes at a time. Although I hadn't seen Dr. Taylor in a while, I was still supposed to keep practicing these things. "Have you been doing your exercises?" Mom asked.

"Yeah."

"Well, think of this experience as part of your ERP."

"ERP is supposed to prepare me for normal, everyday gross experiences. Not for when a four-legged mammal who chews on animal carcasses gets mouth juice on me. Nobody should think that's okay."

Mom smiled and bit her lip.

"What's so funny?" I asked.

"Sorry. I used to let my dog give me kisses all the time when I was your age."

"Really? Why would you do that?"

She handed me a towel. "Because that's how dogs tell you they love you."

I shuddered. Dogs had strange ways of communicating.

And there was no way I was doing a project with them.

Chapter 7

But Dasher and Cubby came over again on Sunday afternoon, just as I finished making an Extra-Fruitie Smoothie for myself. As a chef, I was embarrassed to not have enough for my guests, so I followed Lily's and my Golden Rule: CHB—Chef Hold Back—and served my guests first, even though it meant not getting to try the new recipe myself. I'd just have to read their faces as to whether it was cookbook-worthy.

"Mmmm . . . you're a good smoothie maker," Cubby told me, wiping his mouth with his sweatshirt sleeve. Then he giggled. "Dasher said Luna scared you yesterday."

"Cubby!" Dasher hissed. "Sorry. Luna's just a little friendly."

"I wasn't scared," I said. I opened a canister of Sprinkle-Cake Cookies and they both dug in. "I just had to . . . get home."

"Who's Luna?" Mom asked as she walked in to fill her coffee cup.

"Luna is one of Snowball's pups. And Snowball"—Cubby paused to burp—"raced in the Iditarod."

"Wow," Mom said.

"What's the Iditarod?" I asked.

"Only the coolest sled dog race in Alaska," Cubby said, looking at me like I had asked what cheese was. "Probably the coolest in the world."

"Our dad raced in it twice," Dasher added. "And in the Yukon Quest once."

"Remember, Ana? We saw the Iditarod on the news," Mom said.

Now I remembered. We had watched a segment about it. There was a person who stood on a sled while a bunch of dogs pulled it. It looked cold, scary, and dangerous. All things that didn't sound like fun to me.

"Last year we all went as handlers," Cubby said.

"Handlers?" I asked.

"Someone who helps with the dogs—hooking them up, putting on booties and harnesses, scoopin' poop. It was so much fun." Dasher pulled the straw out of her drink and sucked smoothie from the bottom of it.

Cleaning up doggy poo in the freezing cold—fun? I smiled and nodded, pretending I got it.

"So, we still have to figure out what we're going to do for our Explorations project," Dasher said. "Want to come over?"

"Uh . . ."

Mom smiled at me. "That's a good idea. I need to run some errands, and this way you won't have to come along."

Dasher grabbed a handful of cookies and put them in her coat pocket before heading out.

As we biked to their house, I thought about what Lily might be doing right then. I'd tried calling her that morning, but no one had answered. I pictured Via inviting her over and the two of them speaking in Pig Latin. Via had tried teaching us at lunch, but I couldn't decode it fast enough. Lily could, though, and the two of them had had a whole Pig Latin conversation without me. I couldn't even tell if they were talking about me or not.

When Dasher, Cubby, and I walked into the Hopkinses' backyard, we were greeted by a barking chorus. The dogs were all over the place—some even standing on their doghouses. I stopped and stared. These dogs pulled Mr. Hopkins through the Alaskan wilderness? How did he get them to all run in the same direction? They couldn't even hold still for a minute.

"Do you want to help feed them?" Dasher asked as we walked closer. "It's snack time."

"That's okay. I'll watch."

"Hey, Cubby, can you get the water pail?" Dasher stuck a cookie in her mouth and bent over to uncoil a hose.

"So, want to hear my project idea?" I asked.

"Yeah, one sec though. Lemme just finish up here, or the dogs'll all be whining." Dasher wheeled a huge plastic barrel into one of the dog pens. There was a sign on the gate that said FEMEALS ONLY—NO MEALS ALLOWD.

"What's a 'femeal'?" I asked.

"Female. Cubby made it. We separate the male and female dogs so we don't end up with more dogs."

I nodded. It definitely looked like they didn't need more dogs.

Dasher began filling the dogs' food bowls. As she did, one of the "femeals" came up to the fence—the one that'd slobbered all over me.

Dasher scratched the dog behind its ears. "Hey, Luna. You hungry?" The dog licked its lips. "She wants to say hello to you."

"Hi," I said, giving a quick wave.

"You can feed her if you want. Here, I'll hold her."

"Unless you're still scared," Cubby said, daring me.

"I'm not scared," I said. Not exactly. More worried about germs, but I couldn't tell them that. "Just hold her collar."

I went into the pen, and Dasher dropped some doggie food into my hand. *I can wash afterward*, I told myself.

I stuck my food-filled fist toward Luna, hoping it wouldn't be the last time I'd see my fingers. And that I didn't come down with human heartworm.

Luna sniffed my hand. I reminded myself that, supposedly, dogs' mouths were cleaner than humans'.

I opened my fist. Delicately, she gobbled the food up like a vacuum. It tickled, reminding me of Bernie, and making me forget for a moment where Luna's mouth might have been before she licked me.

Luna's tail waved all over the place, like she was whisking egg whites with it.

"Pet her, if you want," Dasher said.

I leaned over and skimmed my hand down Luna's white-and-black fur. It was thick and warm, which felt good on my chapped hands.

This wasn't so bad. "You can let go of her collar," I told Dasher. Luna lay down at my feet and licked my sneakers. I laughed.

Dasher started filling the food bowls next to each doghouse. As she did, the dogs hurried over and snarfed up the food, each one's tail happily wagging.

Then I noticed one little white snout and set of paws peeking out of a doghouse.

"Who's that?" I asked, pointing.

Dasher looked up. "That's just Sweet Pea." She poured some food into another bowl.

I watched as Sweet Pea finally tiptoed out of her doghouse and over to her food bowl, looking around as if the big bad wolf was lurking around the corner. She was smaller than the rest of the dogs, and one of her ears was folded down more than the other one.

I crept over to Sweet Pea. As I did, Luna finished up her food and came as close to me as her chain would allow so I could pet her. My hands were already dirty anyway, so I patted her before turning back to Sweet Pea.

"Hi," I said and stepped closer, but she fled into her doghouse.

"Don't take it personally," Dasher said. "She doesn't trust people yet. Or dogs, for that matter. They're all too loud and pushy for her."

The dog pen sounded just like middle school. And, like me, Sweet Pea was surrounded by Vias.

"We're not sure what to do with her." Dasher wiped her hands off on her pants. "All done. Should we work on our project now?"

"Yeah, we better," I said. I looked back one last time, but Sweet Pea was hidden away in her doghouse where she was safe. "Bye, Sweet Pea," I whispered.

After I scrubbed up in the Hopkinses' bathroom, we went to the kitchen. Dasher grabbed a juice box from the fridge. "Want one?"

I shook my head. We sat down at the kitchen table.

"Um. I had an idea for our project." I pulled out my recipe binder from my backpack and took a deep breath. "My friend Lily and I have been cooking since we were seven years old. My idea is that you and I could create a cookbook—maybe all desserts—and sell it at school."

Dasher leaned back in her chair until it was on two legs, grabbed a bag of Oreos from the counter behind her, and snapped her chair back into place. "So, I'm not sure I get it. We'd make chocolate chip cookies and sell 'em? No offense, but don't you think Mr. Creed will say it's too simple?"

"We'd be writing and selling cookbooks. And also, they'd be specialty desserts—all original."

"Well, I kind of had my own idea for a project," she said, chewing and swallowing. She had a piece of black cookie lodged in her braces. I focused on the table. "It's called 'A Day in the Life of a Sled Dog Racer.' It'd be about prepping for a sprint race. You could be the dogs' handler."

I began drawing A's into my hand.

"We'd have so much fun training the dogs together!"

"I don't know."

"Seriously: once you start working with the dogs, you'll *love* the sport," she said, smiling with her now-black braces.

"I'll think about it," I said, even though there was no way I would ever consider doing a dribbly dog project.

"Mmmm . . . that smells good," Dad said, walking into the kitchen. "Is whatever it is ready?"

"It's Cucumber-Lemon Bread, but it's still too warm. You'll get the first slice, though."

"Deal. In the meantime . . ." He flipped open the cabinets, looking for something to eat. "How's school going?"

I shook my head and told him about Dasher and our project.

He smiled anyway. "Well, maybe this will give you a chance to branch out—try something you've never done before?"

Had he forgotten who he was talking to? I never branched out.

He pulled a box of crackers off the shelf. "Just be open. New school, new experiences, you know? Remember when your mom wanted you to try asparagus and we had to bribe you with a new spatula just to get you to taste it? Now how many asparagus recipes have you come up with?"

"Six. Asparagus quiche, asparagus-and-Swiss-cheese muffins, asparagus mac and cheese—"

"See? Sometimes it's worth trying something new." He shrugged. "If not that, then maybe instead of telling Dasher what you want to do, you need to show her. Bake her the best batch of cookies you can." He began slicing a piece of bread from the loaf pan.

"Dad, it's still too hot."

"You know that doesn't stop me from supporting your craft," he said, plopping the piece into his hand. "Ouch! Hot, hot, hot!" He juggled the bread from hand to hand until I got out a plate for him to drop it on. "I'll just let that cool a bit."

I rolled my eyes. He never learned.

But he had given me an idea. The next morning after English, I stopped Dasher on her way out the door.

"Here," I said, handing her a baggie of chocolate-blueberry sugar cookies.

"Yum. What're these for?" she asked, digging right in.

"Just enjoy them," I said. I hoped Dad was right.

Chapter 8

After school the next day, Dasher and Cubby stopped by my house again. Dasher and I sat down at my kitchen island, while Cubby played on the living room floor with Bernie.

"So," Dasher said, eating two of the cracker sandwiches I made at once. "I've been thinking about our project, and I have an idea. There's this junior sled dog race I'm training for in Michigan this December: The Sleeping Bear. It's a sprint race. There aren't many around here, so I'm super psyched about it." She guzzled down a glass of my special chocolate and marshmallow s'mores milk. "Wow, that's good."

She continued. "I know—what does this race have to do

with you, right? Well, at every race, there's this breakfast they serve, for the volunteers and spectators."

Cubby nodded.

"So, anyways. You like to cook, right?"

"Yeah . . ."

"You could help with the breakfast thing, and I could do the race—graph speeds, tell about what makes a good sled dog—stuff like that. Our topic would be 'A Day in the Life of a Sled Dog *Race*,' instead of *Racer*."

"What would I do, exactly?" I asked, getting up to serve her some more cracker sandwiches.

"Make tons of pancakes. I've been to lots of race breakfasts for my dad, and they're always shorthanded, the pancakes are awful, and they usually run out. Your cookies and these sandwiches and this milk are super good. You could do the same thing with pancakes, don't you think? You'd be a hit."

"Uh—" I wasn't sure yet whether this was a good thing or not.

"So I'd get to do my sled dog stuff, and you could do your cooking stuff, and then we'd just have to put it together." She stuffed another whole sandwich in her mouth. "So wa oo you fink?"

"Yeah, what do you think?" Cubby asked.

Pancakes were one of my favorite things to make variations of. This could be really cool. But before I could even say yes, my OCD had questions for me: *What if someone gets sick from something you make? Or what if you get sick from being around all those people?*

I must have paused for too long, because Dasher held up her hands. "But if you don't want to," she said, "we can think of something else."

I tapped my chin with my finger. I did practice super-safe cleaning procedures. And I'd be making a difference at the race. They probably just served pancakes made from a box most of the time. "I'll have to check with my parents," I said. "But if they say it's okay, I can write up our proposal for Mr. Creed by tomorrow."

"But we don't have to turn anything in until next week."

"That's okay. I want to get a head start. Can you let the Sleeping Bear people know I'll be a chef for the breakfast? Do you need me to write up a menu of some of the kinds of pancakes I'd be making?" I was already brainstorming possibilities: obviously some with fruit, some with coconut, maybe something spicy . . .

"No, it's not formal like that. They'll just be happy to have someone who knows what they're doing. I'll let 'em know you're helping." Dasher finished off her milk. "So you want to come over today and help me practice for the race?"

I figured I might as well see what sled dog racing was, since I still didn't get it. "Sure."

As we biked, Dasher explained more about the race.

"And I'm going to be one of the handlers," Cubby said, holding onto Dasher's shoulders as he balanced on the bike pegs.

"Have you ever sled dogged, Cubby?" I asked.

He laughed. "You mean mushed? Lots."

"With *one* dog," Dasher explained. "And only Dad's retired ones."

"Muffinhead is real fast though," Cubby told me. "And next winter, Dad'll let me race, too."

Once we got to their house, we went around to the back. "Let's start harnessing them up for a run," Dasher said.

I looked around the empty part of the yard. A sprinkler was watering the sun-scorched lawn. "Um, don't you need snow?"

"You really don't know about racing. No worries." Dasher smiled. "We're *dryland* mushing. With a rig instead of a sled." Dasher pointed to a bike-like thing with one wheel in the front and two in the back. "This is how mushers practice when the weather's no good. Meaning there's no snow."

"Yeah," Cubby piped up. "When'll it snow, anyways?"

I laughed. "In Illinois, you never know. In the fall, it could be cold one day and sunny and eighty degrees the next. I guess it's snowed on Thanksgiving before. But usually it doesn't until December."

Dasher and Cubby exchanged glances. "Wow," Dasher said. "That doesn't give me much time to train on snow. But oh well. Come on."

The three of us went into the female pen. Once we opened the gate, the dogs went wild. As usual, Luna ran right up to me.

"Hi there, Luna," I said. She smiled and wagged her tail. I carefully petted the top of her head, dodging her attempts to lick my hand.

"Not all the dogs get to race," Dasher explained. "I'm still trying to form my team. Right now, I only know one of my lead dogs for sure: Ghost."

At the sound of her name, Ghost perked up and her ears went back.

"I'm not sure of my wheel dogs yet."

"Wheel dogs?"

"They're the ones in the back—right in front of my sled. In the adult classes, there's also swing dogs—or point dogs—which are behind the lead dogs and act as their backups. And then there're the team dogs . . ."

Swing dogs, wheel dogs, hotdogs, it was all the same to me.

"So let's get them hooked up and see how it goes," Dasher said. She took a small notebook out of her pocket. I'd noticed her writing in it whenever Mr. Creed wasn't looking. "Here's who I plan to try out first: Ghost and Dots as lead, and Elvis as wheel. Then I want to try Bambi in Dots's place, and Sugarplum as wheel."

"What about trying Sweet Pea?" I asked, looking over at the dog I'd met the day before. She was cowering from all the commotion, while all the other dogs were trying to get our attention.

Dasher laughed. "Sweet Pea? No, she can't race—she'd bolt at the slightest noise. And anyways, if she did ever want to run, we'd have to change her name."

Cubby nodded like it was obvious.

"Why?"

Dasher laughed. "Because Sweet *Pea* rhymes with *gee*—the word that means *turn right*. She wouldn't know whether to turn right or to come to us. She was such a runt at birth, and so skittish, we knew she'd never be a sled dog. And the name kind of fit."

While Dasher looked at her notebook again, Cubby pulled some hotdogs out of his sweatshirt pocket and gave one to Ghost, who snarfed it up. Dasher looked over. "No, Cubby!"

"Aw, why not?" Cubby whined, passing her another one.

"Not before she's about to run! It'll slow her down. Drop it, Ghost!" But Ghost quickly chewed what was in her mouth and sauntered over to her water dish.

"Here, let me have one," I said to Cubby. "I want to give it to Sweet Pea."

Dasher shrugged her shoulders. "You can try, but she probably won't take it from you."

Using a tissue from my pocket, I took a hotdog from Cubby. I kept the meat high in the air as I passed the other dogs and stood near her doghouse. "Here, Sweet Pea."

She froze, but her eyes cautiously followed me. "It's okay." As I put the hotdog in front of her, she backed away. "Come on, girl," I said. Why was she so timid?

Before Sweet Pea could eat the hotdog, another dog jumped up and snatched it. "Peppermint!" Cubby said, laughing.

"Do you have another?" I asked Cubby.

"Nah. That was the last one."

I looked sadly at Sweet Pea. I had a feeling that wasn't the first time she had missed out.

"All right, let's get started," Dasher said, all businesslike. I said goodbye to Sweet Pea and followed Dasher as she got the male dogs out of their pen.

Dasher showed me how they walked the dogs from their doghouses to something called a drop chain. Then I watched her harness and attach each dog to the rig by all sorts of strings.

"Wow, that looks complicated," I said. "Don't you get confused? I'd end up accidentally attaching myself to those ropes."

"You mean lines," Cubby said.

"Eh, you get used to it," Dasher said. "Ana, you can ride your bike next to the dogs and make sure the neck lines and tug lines don't get tangled." Dasher pointed to a bunch of strings that looked like long licorice whips.

"What about me?" Cubby asked.

"You can go back in the house, I guess."

"But I'm a handler."

"Last time you biked next to the dogs, you distracted them, and they couldn't hear my commands." Then Dasher grinned. "I know. Why don't you get the treats for when they're done?"

"Okay!" Cubby started skipping to the house.

Picking out treats actually sounded like fun to me, but I needed to focus on learning more about dog sledding, or sled dogging, or whatever you called it if I wanted this project to work.

"All set," Dasher said, checking the last dog. "Cubby," she yelled, "tell Mom I'm ready."

"Why me?" he shouted back.

"Because you're my handler."

"Fine." Cubby stomped away.

Dasher turned to me. "We have to tell Mom whenever we're on a sled. House rule." She put on a helmet and hopped onto the rig. "Ready?" I put on my own bike helmet and nodded.

"Hike," she said, and the two dogs in the front started moving, followed by the one in the back. Dasher began rolling along. I was so busy watching, I forgot to start pedaling.

"Catch up!" Dasher called to me, and I sped up until I was next to them.

The dogs were fast. And they looked like they were having fun.

Dasher kept calling out "Gee" or "Haw," which made them turn right or left.

We circled the yard in a large, wiggly oval shape. Once they really got moving, I couldn't keep up, even pedaling as fast as I could.

"All right, team. Whoa," Dasher said, slowing down the rig until they stopped.

I caught up and braked, catching my breath.

"That was so cool!" I said.

Just then, Cubby shouted from the barn, "Treats are here!" He held up a bag of treats.

"Cubby! No!" Dasher yelled as the dogs got a second wind and made a dash toward Cubby. Taken by surprise, Dasher slipped off the back of the rig and onto the ground!

I gasped.

But she got up, ran after the rig, and jumped back on. "Whoa!" she cried, and the team stopped when they reached Cubby.

"Are you okay?" I asked, clutching my heart and running over. "Do you want me to get your mom?"

"No, I'm good. Most important rule of mushing: you never leave your team," she said, like it wasn't that big of a deal. She didn't even seem to notice that her hoodie and pants were covered in dirt.

"They look so cute with their tongues hanging out!" I said, watching as the dogs chowed down on treats and then grinned, still panting.

"Good observation," Dasher said, looking at each one carefully. "They're too hot. We have to stop for today—they can't practice much in this heat," she said.

"Heat? It's not even sixty out."

"That's hot to a sled dog. They need cold weather. Like, below zero. Let's get 'em some water." Dasher pulled a hose over to where the team was resting. Cubby got out water dishes, I filled them up, and then we walked the dogs back to their pens and attached them to their spinners. By the time we finished, I was sweaty and even had a couple pieces of dirt under my fingernails. I'd probably have to throw out my nailbrush after I cleaned up.

"If you want to help again, I'm gonna practice tomorrow," Dasher told me while taking weights out of the rig.

I looked down at my grimy hands again. I hadn't touched

actual dirt since third grade or so, when my OCD started to take over my thoughts.

"You okay?" Dasher asked.

"Yeah, I'm fine," I said. "I'll be here tomorrow."

A week later, Mr. Creed handed back our Explorations proposal. At the top of the paper he'd written, in red pen, "The two of you need to collaborate more—your teamwork counts for one quarter of your grade. Ms. Morgan will need to be more active in the responsibilities associated with the sled dog racing, such as helping to train and care for the dogs. Ms. Hopkins will need to learn and master the recipes used for the breakfast, and create at least one of her own."

Help care for the dogs? I hoped that didn't include anything involving mouths, noses, or rears.

Dasher skimmed the paper and handed it back to me. "Well, that shouldn't be that hard," she said. "I make Eggos and stuff all the time."

We were in worse shape than I thought.

"Eeks," Lily said when I told her about Mr. Creed's comments over lunch. "You want me to help? My aunt used to have a dog."

"Maybe. But it's not just that. He wants Dasher to help with the pancakes, but she's never made anything. Well, I take that back—she considers putting a frozen disc in the toaster cooking."

"That counts as cooking at my house, too," Via said, eating a turkey sandwich from the local sub shop. "My mom never cooks. Right, Lily?"

My mouth dropped open. How many times had Lily been to Via's house?

"You can teach her, Ana," Lily said. "Remember when you taught me how to make meringue? And how to get cookie dough on a cookie sheet without touching it with my fingers?"

We smiled at each other. I had forgotten all about that. It was good to know Lily remembered. "Did you guys decide what you're doing for your project?" I asked, opening my carton of milk. Maybe they had realized there was nothing they could agree on and would both work with someone else.

"Well, it's between something with kids and cooking," Via answered matter-of-factly. "Of course Lily wants to do something with cooking, but—"

"Cooking? What does that mean?" I asked. But I already knew. It had to mean using a cookbook—the one Lily and I had been working on for over a year. I began drawing A's into my hand.

"Or we can combine the two," Via continued. "Like recipes for kids and babies. Didn't you guys make baby brownies?"

Seriously? "Can I talk to you for a minute, Lily?" I asked as calmly as my racing heart would allow.

As we left the table, I began, "You're going to use *our* cookbook recipes with *her*? How could you do that to me?"

"Oh, it's not like that, Ana. I'd never—"

"You said we were still best friends. And then you *steal* all my recipes?"

"*Your* recipes? I made a lot of them, too," she said, pointing to herself.

"Yeah, but now you and Via will get all the credit for *our* hard work."

"You know I wouldn't do that."

I put my hands on my hips. "But *you and Via* would."

"Whatever, Ana. Just . . . chill. Via's not out to get you."

I opened my mouth and then closed it. I couldn't think of a response to that.

"And anyway," she continued, "weren't *you* going to use our recipes for your and Dasher's project if you had your way? You know you would have."

I huffed. "Have fun cooking with your new best friend." I turned and walked off.

I looked at the clock on the cafeteria wall. Lunch wouldn't end for another eight minutes—and I still hadn't finished eating.

I dragged my feet on the way back to the table to get my lunch before Lily got there.

"What happened?" Via asked, unwrapping the cookie that

came with her store-bought sub. She couldn't even make her own cookies, and she was going to get credit for my recipes?

"Enjoy your Explorations project," I said, holding my head high and turning away before the tears started.

Since we weren't allowed to leave the cafeteria, I went into the bathroom and tried to wash away the fight from my hands, but the soap was useless.

"Just chill?" Did Lily really say that to me? She even *sounded* like Via now. And there wasn't anything I could do about it.

It was the longest eight minutes ever.

Chapter 9

Saturday morning, I woke up drained. I had spent the whole night replaying the fight with Lily in my head. Not only were we no longer on speaking terms—she was also going to steal all my recipes. Now she and Via would be the ones appearing on a cooking network, Via telling everyone how she came up with *my* recipes.

When I explained the whole situation to Bernie, he squeaked in shock. Then he sneezed.

"Bless you. And the worst part is, now I have nowhere to sit at lunch."

He sneezed again.

"Plus, Dasher's on her way over, and I have to teach her how to make pancakes. *Gourmet* pancakes."

I could tell Bernie was too speechless for squeaks.

The doorbell rang. "Wish us luck," I said.

"So, how long do you think this will take?" Dasher asked as I led her into the kitchen. "It's supposed to get down to fifty degrees today—I might be able to get in a longer practice for the Sleeping Bear race. You can come over to help hook the dogs up and cool them off afterward, if you want."

"Let's get through the pancakes first," I said. I laid out simple ingredients and a few specialty ones: cinnamon, coconut, chocolate chips, and grated carrots.

"Carrots? Did your mom tell you to use those?" Dasher said, making a face. "Moms are all about the healthy."

"I was thinking of carrot cake," I replied. "I thought we could try the same thing with pancakes."

"Cool." She opened the bag of chocolate chips and poured some into her hand.

"Whoa. Stop!" I shrieked and grabbed the bag from her a little more forcefully than I meant to. "Sorry. I just have some rules we need to follow." I quickly told her some of the basics of cooking: hand and counter sanitation, washing the outside of the eggs, and never sampling anything.

"Wow, I don't know if my mom does any of those things," Dasher said. "Don't you ever want to just, like, stick your finger in cookie dough and eat it or anything?"

"No, never," I said with a firm shake of my head.

That wasn't exactly true. When I was little, I used to sample things I was making—even cookie dough—and I remembered that it tasted really good. But in third grade, we learned all about germs. We watched a video about germs and did an activity where the germs on our hands glowed in UV light. That night, when I was trying to sleep, I imagined all of the germs in my room glowing—and I was horrified. Everything was covered in germs.

When my germ obsession first started, Mom told me I could wash my toys and hands if it bothered me. But then I started washing stuff all the time.

Soon, I couldn't touch anything without panicking. It got so bad, I didn't want to eat because I'd be putting germy food in my mouth. That's when Mom and Dad made me start seeing Dr. Taylor.

Although I'd gotten a lot better since then, I knew too much about raw eggs and salmonella to ever eat raw cookie dough again.

I sighed. "Let's just get started. Here's the recipe for Carrot Pancakes with a Cream Cheese Glaze that I came up with."

I opened up my binder to show her. "The glaze is pretty complicated because it needs to be the right consistency," I explained. "Why don't we start the pancakes together, and then you can watch me make the glaze?"

Dasher looked at her watch. "How 'bout I make the pancakes while you make the glaze, to save time?" she said. "I've seen my mom make pancakes before."

"I guess," I said. "Go ahead and wash up, and then we can begin."

As she dried her hands, Dasher read the recipe from my binder. "All right. One cup flour." She looked up. "Like, what size cup?"

"Huh?" I asked.

"Well, there's those tiny cups you use to rinse your mouth at the dentist, and then there's the ginormous ones used for soda at gas stations—"

"Don't you measure out food for your dogs?"

"Yeah. With a coffee mug."

I nodded and turned to look for a measuring cup, trying to hide the horror on my face.

The smoke detector went off just as I was returning from the basement fridge with another carton of milk for the glaze.

"It's okay!" Dasher said, fanning the smoky air with my binder. "Our pancakes just got a little overcooked."

"Everyone all right?" Dad asked, rushing in from his office.

Dasher pointed to the griddle, where our blackened pancakes were steaming away. "Sorry, totally my bad," she said, still trying to get the detector to stop as Dad got out a step stool to unplug the battery. "I dropped the bag of chocolate chips all over the floor. As I was picking them up, I forgot to check on the pancakes. They, uh, kind of stuck to the griddle."

We weren't even using chocolate chips in the recipe—I was pretty sure she was just eating them. I wondered if she put the floor ones back in the bag. I made a mental note to toss the bag of chocolate chips later.

"That's okay," I said. "I've burned things before." I looked over my recipe, trying to figure out why they burned so quickly. "Maybe we needed to add more butter."

"I was supposed to add butter?" Dasher said, shaking out more chocolate chips from the bag into her hand. "These are so complicated!"

Once Dasher had left, the pancakes were in the trash, and the griddle was finally useable again, it hit me—I was friendless. I had pulled out my phone to text Lily about what an awful cook Dasher was. But then I remembered we weren't talking.

My phone was silent until Sunday afternoon, when I got a text. *Please be Lily*, I thought. *Please.*

It was Dasher. She wanted to know if I'd bike over and help her try some different dogs for her team.

"Why not? I have nothing else to do," I told Bernie. He sneezed in response.

I biked over and met Dasher by the barn. Cubby ran out of the house to join us, all bundled up in a huge winter coat, snow boots, and mittens. He looked like a giant puffball. I bit my lip to keep from laughing.

"Cubby, what are you doing? It's fifty degrees out," Dasher asked.

"I thought we should practice like it's the real race," Cubby said.

"You're not even in it."

Cubby looked down at his furry boots.

Dasher sighed. "Fine. Go get the rig ready."

Cubby grinned and ran off.

Before we started, I went into Sweet Pea's pen to say hello. When she saw me, she hurried into her doghouse. I dropped some kibble on the ground for her, but she just waited until I left before eating it.

Dasher's dad came out to the dog yard as Dasher was trying to decide which dogs to use.

"Remember, you're only as fast as your slowest dog," Mr. Hopkins told her. "I'd scrap Tulip if I were you." Dasher nodded and pulled out her notebook again as we walked off.

"Want me to ride my bike next to you, like I did last time?" I asked as we walked to the barn.

"You could, but Mr. Creed wants you to be more involved," Dasher said.

"What else is there for me to do besides mushing the dogs myself?" I joked.

"Wanna see what it's like?" Dasher asked, her eyes sparkling.

"What do you mean?"

She smiled. "Get your helmet. You're going to ride with me."

After Dasher, her dad, and I attached the dogs to the rope they pull with, called the gang line, she unzipped the sled bag on the front of the rig. "Hop in."

"Um . . ."

Dasher looked at my face and nodded. "It's a brand-new bag." She pulled open the sides to prove it. "See?"

Her dad held on to one of the front dogs' collars as Dasher helped me get inside. I hoped Dasher didn't notice my legs shaking like gelatin.

"There," she said, smiling as if this would be fun. "You're all set. Ready?"

"Don't go too fast," I blurted out.

She nodded.

Then I looked at the dogs. "Don't go too fast," I said again. The wheel dog, Sugarplum, looked back at me and wagged her tail.

After everyone was in place, Dasher shouted, "Hike!"

Her dad let go, and I held onto the bag for dear life. My heart started to race. This was going to be a disaster!

But all the complicated strings—or lines—attached to the dogs straightened out into an organized web. The dogs stayed in their places. I thought they'd jerk the rig, but the ride actually felt pretty smooth. Kind of like riding a bike—if the bike were dog-powered.

But what if the dogs decided they didn't want to run anymore and some stopped, while some kept going? The sled bag would be propelled through the air and I'd slingshot off the rig at a dangerous speed. What if one of the dogs spotted a squirrel on one side and another dog spotted something else on the other side? I'd be split in two! Maybe Dasher had never thought of that. Maybe I should say something?

I bit my lip. *Just chill.*

So far, all the dogs were just looking forward, their heads bobbing up and down while their legs kicked up dirt.

"You okay?" Dasher asked as we circled their yard.

I concentrated on what the dogs were doing, as if I controlled their focus on their task. Regardless, they had better concentration than most of the kids in my school. After a pause, I said, "Yes."

"Okay. Here's where the fun begins," she replied.

I gulped as we slowed back down next to the barn. I had a feeling what Dasher categorized as fun was different than what I did.

"We're ready, Dad," she said.

Mr. Hopkins got on his four-wheeler and lined up behind us. "Hike up!" Dasher commanded the dogs, and they began to move a little faster.

I was praying we wouldn't be jumping over obstacles or anything. I gripped the sled bag tighter.

Dasher told the dogs to haw (go left), and we snaked through the forest along the dirt path.

I saw a squirrel in a tree and closed my eyes at the thought of what would happen next, but the dogs just kept going.

I loosened my hands a little bit on the bag and looked around. Trees were whizzing past. Wow, my dog's eye view of the forest was pretty cool. They really knew what they were doing. To think, a bunch of dogs were my chauffeurs.

Sunlight peeked through branches of trees as tall as

skyscrapers. I could only imagine what it would be like to do this in the winter. It was probably so pretty with all the snow sparkling like the world was covered in coconut.

Maybe sled dog racing wasn't so crazy after all.

Monday came too fast, and I walked as slowly as possible from my locker to the cafeteria at lunchtime. Where would I sit, now that Lily wasn't my friend anymore?

As I went into the cafeteria, I saw Lily carrying her lunch tray to her regular table. She stopped when she saw me—it looked like maybe she was going to say something.

Apologize, please, I pleaded in my mind. *Then we can be friends again.*

But just then, Via walked over to her. "OMG. Guess who wants to ask me to the Halloween dance!" She grabbed Lily's arm and off they went.

I held my head high and walked right by their table like I had somewhere to go. Even though I had brought water flavored with cucumber slices from home, I got in the lunch line to stall by buying a milk.

Dasher was two people ahead of me in line. "Hey, Ana," she said. "Tough quiz in English, huh? What'd you get?"

"Six out of six," I said.

"Wow, I only got two right." She picked up a lunch plate with something like chop suey on it. "We didn't have quizzes on being respectful at my old school. And now my mom is making me study, since I'm doing so bad on them." The cashier handed her back some change, which she stuck in her back pocket. "Well, I guess I'll see you later."

"Bye."

I paid for my useless milk with nickels so I could eat up even more lunch time counting them out.

But then I couldn't stall any longer—I had to figure out where to sit. At one table, a bunch of boys showed each other gross concoctions they had mixed together in their mouths. Another table was already crowded. My stomach growled.

I looked over at Lily and Via. They were laughing and eating like I had never even sat with them.

I wondered if Lily had shared my Marshmallow & Chocolate Dip recipe with Via already. No way could I sit within a ten-foot radius of them. I smoothed down my hair, my skin crawling as though everyone was watching me. I couldn't just go up to someone and ask if I could sit at their table.

And then I saw Dasher, sitting alone like always. She waved. Taking a deep breath, I walked over.

Chapter 10

"I made you a special veggie sandwich," I told Bernie, dropping an extra leaf of lettuce from my Green-Salad Sandwich into his cage.

Instead of running over to it like he normally did, he sat in the corner and looked up at me. "Not hungry today?" I asked him. "Or just tired?" Neither of us liked Monday mornings very much.

It had been a week since Lily and I had fought. I kept hoping she'd text me, but she hadn't. I still followed her on Facebook though. Yesterday, she had updated her status to say, I'm wearing purple nail polish and a lavender shirt. Stylish or a fashion no-no?

Via had responded, Stylish! Your fashion sense is rockin'.

Lily was way more into fashion than I was. And if Via knew what was stylish, or rockin', or whatever—well, no wonder Lily wanted to be friends with her and not me.

"Ana, you need to get going," Mom yelled from downstairs. "You're running late today. Need any help?"

"No, I'm coming," I shouted back.

I patted Bernie's head. "Gotta go. Let's hope Lily apologizes today. See you after school!"

I checked my phone one last time. Still nothing.

"Good morning, class," Mr. Creed said as the first-period bell rang to start the day.

"Good morning, Mr. Creed," we mumbled back.

"Today, you and your partner will be writing a status report on your progress for your Explorations project. You may begin."

Dasher and I had been working on our project for a long time now. I had become an expert at helping to get the dogs into their harnesses, wrapping up all the lines after they ran, and filling their food bowls. Dasher had me take pictures of her practice runs, too.

We had also been trying out different pancake recipes. I had learned to give Dasher one task at a time, like stirring the batter, and then watch her do it. I was still working on teaching her how to do things like crack an egg or measure flour properly.

"Can't we just toss ingredients in, like they do on cooking shows?" she'd asked. But after she tried it once with the flour and created a stiff ball of pancake batter, she started measuring and leveling off ingredients like me.

As class went on, we wrote about how we had chosen Dasher's team for the race: Ghost, Dots, and Elvis, and how they had improved their speed.

Then we included information on our pancake recipes for the volunteer breakfast. I wrote down the varieties we were thinking of serving: carrot cake (I had tried them again on my own), basil, and lavender.

"Any race I've been to, all I ate were plain old pancakes and bacon," Dasher said as we turned our report in. "Glad it's not me making these. They look way hard."

"Maybe," I said, "but they're nothing like racing."

Dasher shook her head and laughed.

At lunch, I decided I was going to be the bigger person and clear things up between Lily and me.

I looked over at my old table. Lily was already there. And Via wasn't. Once I got my lunch, I'd go up to Lily and get the full story. Maybe it was just a misunderstanding. She and Via probably weren't doing a cookbook. Lily wouldn't let them.

As I was standing in line for a taco, Via tapped me on the back.

"Hey, long time no see," she said. "Where've you been?"

"Uh, hi," I replied and turned back to order my specialty taco. "A flour tortilla with cheese—Chihuahua, if you have it. No lettuce, tomato, or meat. But do you have any lime wedges or white beans?"

"Huh?" the cafeteria lady asked. This is one of the reasons why I rarely ate cafeteria food.

"For flavor and texture."

"This isn't a made-to-order restaurant," she said like I'd asked for lobster tail. She shoved my sad tortilla with a light sprinkling of faux cheese at me.

"Wow, you sure are high maintenance," Via said, grabbing a stale-looking cookie from the dessert basket. "Do you, like, cut your candy bars with a knife and fork, too?"

I held in a gasp. The only people who knew I did that were my parents and Lily.

"Two twenty-five," the cashier interrupted.

I paid for my taco without looking back at Via, and charged over to Lily's table.

"Hi, Ana," Lily said, looking surprised to see me. "Are you—"

"I cannot believe you told her!"

"Told who what?" she asked.

"Via." I leaned in closer so no one else would hear. "About how I eat my candy bars with a fork and a knife. Did you tell her about my OCD, too?"

"I never—"

And then I saw it—a plastic cup of red Jell-O in front of her. Her eyes followed my gaze.

"Ana, Via brought an extra, and I didn't—"

"How could you? I thought I could trust you." Out of the corner of my eye, I could see Via walking over. "Never again."

I stomped away. Not only had Lily lied about telling Via my secret, but they were celebrating that their table was "Ana-free" with squishy red foods! It felt like I had been slapped in the face.

I plopped my tray down on Dasher's table, my hands shaking.

"Are you okay?" she asked. "You look like you just got coal in your Christmas stocking."

"I wish."

"Be right back—I forgot to get a spork," Dasher said, getting up.

I sat alone at the table, drawing A's into my hand.

Lily and I were through.

I could make new friends . . . couldn't I? I didn't need her.

But Lily was the only one who knew everything about me. And she used to make sure it stayed that way.

"For your information," she once told a boy in elementary school who was teasing me, "it's because of your cootie breath that she even has to wash her backpack straps."

Of course, everyone standing around thought what she said was hysterical, but he didn't bug me again. I didn't tell Lily that

I *had* kind of worried about the boy's cootie breath dripping onto my backpack.

Now I had no one at school to defend me if something happened. And who was I scared would tease me now? Via. The same girl Lily traded me in for.

I didn't need her—there were plenty of girls at Jefferson I could be friends with.

But Lily not only was my protector, she was super fun. We liked the same movies, watched the same TV shows, and, of course, we were both crazy about baking and cooking.

I looked around the cafeteria for possibilities. But everyone was already part of a group, or way too different from me.

Forget it. There was no way I could tell someone about my OCD anyway. With Lily, we were friends before it started. Now, I'd either have to explain what it was to the person, or I'd have to hide it. And if I didn't tell them, they might be really sloppy with their cleaning habits. I'd be better off with no friends than germy ones.

I swallowed. My throat was sore from trying not to cry.

No. I needed to concentrate on my pancake recipes and helping out Dasher with the race—I didn't have time for friends.

But if Lily called right then to apologize (and promised to never speak to Via again *and* to make her to sit at a different lunch table), I knew I'd definitely think about forgiving her.

Days passed without Lily apologizing. Would we ever make up?

Not if Via had anything to do with it. I was sure she was happy to not have me at their table anymore. Every day, I saw them talking and laughing over the cafeteria food.

At least I had my Explorations project to keep me busy. After school on Monday, I biked to Dasher's, like always.

Dasher was opening a box on the ground as I walked over to her. Inside were three huge plastic bags, labeled SMALL, MEDIUM, and LARGE. She ripped open the SMALL bag.

"Wow, that's a lot of socks," I said. There had to be over a hundred, all different colors and patterns.

"You mean booties. They're to protect the dogs' feet in the snow," Dasher said. "This isn't even all of them. We're supposed to get more next month."

"Why so many?" I pictured Dasher and Cubby handing them out to trick-or-treaters at Halloween, not knowing that around here, we passed out candy.

"They're for my dad's dogs, too." Dasher dug around in the bag, pulling out four black-and-green ones.

"Yeah, his dogs went through seventeen hundred booties in the Iditarod," Cubby told me.

"You mean seventeen," I said.

"No, seventeen *hundred*."

"He's right," Dasher said. "They wear out fast. And each dog needs four booties, and my dad's team has sixteen dogs, which is . . . a lot of booties changed at checkpoints."

"They're so cute," I said, pointing to a light pink one.

"I guess." Dasher used her teeth to tear open the MEDIUM bag.

Cubby, Dasher, and I tried different-sized booties on Ghost, Dots, and Elvis. Cubby even put a pair on his stuffed bear, Noodles.

"Cool. We're all set for when it snows," Dasher said, undoing the Velcro on Elvis's farm-animal booties. "Now, I also need to practice bagging a dog today."

"Bagging a dog?"

"If a dog gets tired or injured, I need to put 'em in the dog bag on the sled. Dad has me practice with a big thing of dog food since the dogs hate getting in the bag. Wanna time me?"

"Sure."

Dasher got a bag of dog food out of the barn. It had paper eyes, a nose, and a tongue glued on the front. She put the dog-faced dog-food bag on a rolling cart, walked down the trail a ways, and set it on the ground. Then she ran back.

"The dog is in place," she said.

We harnessed and attached Dasher's team to the gang line. She then got on the rig. "Begin timing when I stop the rig."

Dasher and her team took off down the trail. When she got to the "injured dog," I started the stopwatch.

She tied the rope called a snub line to a tree to keep the team from running away. Then she jumped off the rig and went over to bag. She bent down as if she were looking it over, then ran back to the sled bag and unzipped it.

Dasher picked up the "dog" and placed it into the sled bag. Then she zipped it up, got back onto the rig, and released the snub line. Once she began moving again, I stopped the timer.

She turned her team and circled back to me. "How'd I do?"

"Six minutes, thirteen seconds."

She made a face. "I want to shave at least ninety seconds off that," she said. "I'll keep practicing."

Dasher ran through the whole practice a couple more times until she was down to four minutes, fifty-seven seconds. "We can work on it again tomorrow," she said.

"I want to try," Cubby said.

"No, Cubby. I need to get the dogs back in their pens."

"You never let me do anything!" he yelled, then ran into the house.

"Whatever," Dasher said and rolled her eyes.

Just then, Mrs. Hopkins pulled up in the driveway. "Dana Hopkins, what are you doing out here without me home? And did you finish your homework?"

"Almost."

"No dogs until it's done," her mom said and went into the house. It reminded me of my parents not letting me cook when my hands were bad from washing them too much.

Dasher sighed. "I flunked my math test and a bunch of those English quizzes, and now Mom's on me all the time about my homework."

"Can I stay and play with Sweet Pea?" I asked.

"Dasher, *now*," her mom called through the window.

"Yeah—take her for a walk. I'll be done in a half hour or so. We could do something afterward."

"Like bake?" I said.

She shrugged. "I guess. See you in thirty." Dasher went into the house.

I let myself into the female pen. While the other dogs were pawing at a ball and running back and forth, playing together as much as their chains would allow, Sweet Pea sat in her doghouse and watched. Why didn't she want to play with the other dogs? They all seemed to get along. And they all had a purpose. It was just Sweet Pea who was lonely and didn't have a job pulling a sled.

"Wanna go for a walk?" I asked her, waving a leash in my hand. No response. I tiptoed to where she stood, frozen. "It's okay."

Her ears flipped back against her head.

"It's okay," I said again, and she seemed to relax a little. "Good girl." I petted her with one hand while clipping the leash onto her collar with the other. "Come on."

Sweet Pea pepped up a little with the leash on, sniffing around as I took her out of her pen. She was actually walking with me—I got her to trust me! "Let's go."

Sniff, sniff, sniff. Pull, pull, pull. Sniff, sniff, sniff. Sweet Pea stopped to smell everything as we walked, pulling on the leash.

"Thatta girl," I said. She really seemed to like walking. I picked up my pace a little bit, and she followed along. I slowed, and so did she. "Hm," I said, "maybe you'd be a better sled dog than people think."

If only I could convince Dasher to let her run.

The Hopkinses' kitchen was so different from mine, with its old cabinets, a black-and-white checkered floor, and what looked to be a homemade wooden table. And there were little ceramic dogs everywhere. Even their cookie jar was shaped like a dog. The plates next to the sink had paintings of dogs on them. I wondered if those were their fancy plates. The whole thing looked like one of those "before" kitchens on home makeover shows. I always liked the befores better, anyway—they were much more homey.

Since we hadn't decided what to make yet, I pulled my binder out of my backpack and showed Dasher some new recipes I had come up with.

"Wow, I'd be scared to make up my own recipe," she said. "Especially after that pancake ball I made the other day."

"Lily and I do it all the time," I said. "I mean, we used to." I bit my lip.

"Who's Lily again?"

"Oh . . . she was my friend. We kind of went our separate ways, though. But she liked to bake, too." I told her about the edible Monopoly game Lily and I had made at Grammy's once. "We had frosted graham crackers for the game board and decorated the whole thing with candies. We had to look everywhere for different-colored fruit leathers to use as hotel squares." I smiled, but then frowned. That was when we were still friends.

Now I could picture Via in my place, attaching blue-raspberry fruit leathers to the Monopoly board.

I shook the thought out of my head. "So what do you want to make?" I asked, excited that I didn't need Lily to make up a recipe anymore.

"Something basic," Dasher said. "And *not* pancakes."

DASHER & ANA'S SANDY BEACH ICE CREAM

1 tsp cinnamon
2 tbsp sugar
1 pint vanilla ice cream

1. Wipe down countertop. Wash hands thoroughly.
2. In a small bowl, mix together cinnamon and sugar. Set aside.
3. With a clean ice cream scooper, scoop ice cream into three perfect balls. Do not let your hands touch the sides of the ice cream container.
4. Wrap each ice cream ball in plastic wrap and put them back in freezer to refreeze. Clean up your workspace.
5. Once ice cream has refrozen, wash hands again and remove ice cream from freezer. Unwrap the plastic wrap and drop one ice cream ball into the bowl of cinnamon and sugar. Gently, roll the ice cream around with a spoon until completely covered. Place in a fun bowl.
6. Repeat with the other two balls. Share immediately.

Chapter 11

"I'll write up a copy of the recipe for you," I told Dasher after we finished eating our ice cream. "If you want it, that is." I planned to leave out some of my tips she might not understand.

"You write a lot about washing up and cleaning stuff," she said, looking over my shoulder at the recipe.

Uh-oh. She thought I was weird—I knew it. I smoothed my ponytail. "I, uh—"

"It's so thorough! You're an awesome cook."

I breathed a sigh of relief. Thorough was good.

"I have an idea notebook, too. But mine has stuff about sled dogs." Dasher went in the other room and came back with the book I'd seen her draw in before. She showed me what she'd been working on: lists of possible dog teams, what to pack in the sled, and maps she drew of different routes to try.

"Wow," I said. "You're a good artist."

She blushed. "So are you—but with food."

I smiled.

"So, did you hear about the Halloween party?" Dasher asked.

I had totally forgotten that it was almost Halloween. My stomach lurched as I remembered that, without Lily, I was officially without anyone to go to the party with—and without a costume.

"It sounds like so much fun!" Dasher continued. "My old school's parties were pretty boring. Did I ever tell you about my old school? It was so small that kindergarten through fifth grade was in one classroom, and six through twelfth grade was in the other. One year for Halloween we combined both classes to play games, but that only made twenty of us. Jefferson's party will be huge! And there's gonna be games and a DJ."

"I might go," I said. "I'm not sure yet."

The back door opened, and Mrs. Hopkins came in.

"Hi, Mommy!" Cubby said, following her into the kitchen.

"You two practicing your pancake recipes?" she asked, filling the coffee pot.

"No, just something for fun," Dasher said. She was bent over one of her maps, adding some detail.

Mrs. Hopkins walked to the garbage to dump out the old coffee filter. As she flipped open the garbage lid, her eyes widened. "Why are there so many paper towels in here?"

Cubby ran over. "That's like a whole roll!"

Mrs. Hopkins looked confused. "What happened?"

I looked at Dasher and swallowed hard.

"Oh. I accidentally spilled ice cream and sugar all over the floor," Dasher answered without hesitating. "I had to clean it up."

"I better go," I said, grabbing my binder and putting it into my backpack. "Thanks for . . . everything, Dasher. See you later."

On my way out, I said goodbye to Sweet Pea. Although she stayed in her doghouse, she almost sniffed my hand.

My heart felt like dough rising.

As I reached my house, I could see Mom's shadow through the window, like she was waiting for me. *Strange*, I thought with a shiver.

When I walked in the front door, Mom's shoulders dropped, and she motioned for me to sit on the couch with her.

"What's wrong?" I asked, sliding my backpack off and sitting down next to her.

"I don't know how to tell you this," Mom said, pausing. She grabbed a tissue and dabbed at her eyes. "It's Bernie . . ."

I put my hand over my mouth. I couldn't ask. I didn't have to.

Mom went on. "When I went into your room to get the laundry, I found him in the corner of his cage. He wasn't moving."

I sat up straight. "Not moving? What did you do? Did you have to give him CPR?"

"No, honey. It was too late."

"You mean he . . ."

She nodded.

"But what happened? Was he hurt?" My stomach felt like it had dropped down into my shoes.

She shook her head and reached for another tissue. "It didn't look like it."

I gasped. "Oh no. He had been sniffling. Just a little. I thought maybe he had gotten an allergy to something."

"He was pretty old for a guinea pig. And you took excellent care of him." Mom put her hand on my arm. "He probably just died of old age."

I shrugged her off. "But you should have called me at school, or at Dasher's. Why didn't you call me?" I hit the couch pillow with my hand.

"Sweetie, there was nothing you could have done for him. He left this world a very happy guinea pig."

"We could've taken him to the vet right when I noticed him sneezing. And he could've gotten better. Is he still in his cage?" I asked.

"After I found him, I brought him to the vet."

"Did you bring his favorite toy?" Bernie had a miniature cowbell that he loved to pick up and ring. I leapt off the couch and ran to my room.

"Ana—" Mom called out as she followed.

104

Bernie's cage was gone. So were all of his belongings. "You threw everything away already? Even his bell?"

"I brought his bell with him to the vet's." Mom shook her head and started to cry again. "But I thought his empty cage in your room would upset you, so I took it out. I'm so sorry. I can bring it back in if it would make you feel better. Losing a pet can be so hard." She walked over to give me a hug.

"But I didn't get to say goodbye," I said, pulling away to grab a tissue.

Mom sighed sadly. "I know, I know." She sat down on my bed, and patted the spot beside her.

We sat in silence for a few minutes. "Try to remember the happy times you had with Bernie," Mom said. "You gave him a wonderful life." She kissed the top of my head. "Why don't you call Lily to come over?"

I shook my head.

"Maybe I should call Dr. Taylor?" she said.

"Don't. Please?"

"All right. Just rest for a bit, and I'll come get you when dinner's ready. Unless you'd like me to sit with you? Keep you company?"

"I'm not tired. I'm not hungry. I just want to be alone." I buried my head in my pillow.

"Okay. I'll have your dad check on you when he gets home. I'm really sorry. Bernie was a good little guy. I'm going miss him, too." She patted my shoulder and left.

I cried and cried until there was nothing left inside of me.

I was completely hollow. Every time I thought I had gotten myself together, I pictured Bernie's smiling face looking up at me like he always did when I got home from school, as if he were saying, "You're home! Let's play!" Now I'd never see him again. There was just an empty space in my room.

I drew A's into my hand. *What if I had told Mom that Bernie seemed sick when I first noticed? Then he could've taken some medicine and gotten better. What if I'd come home right after school instead of going to Dasher's? I could've found him in time to rush him to the vet. Why did I go to Dasher's?*

A, A, A, I drew in my hand.

I really wanted to call Lily, but I just couldn't do it. So I did the next best thing.

"Hello, who's there?"

"Grammy, it's Ana," I said through my tears.

"What is it, honey? Is everybody all right?"

"No, it's Bernie. He . . . he . . . died."

"Oh, dear," she said. "I'm sorry. I know how close you were to him."

"He was fine. And then his nose started getting runny, and I didn't do anything! I didn't take him to the vet. Instead, I went to school and then to Dasher's to work on a stupid school project. I didn't know he was so sick."

"Of course not, dear. How could you? You're being too hard on yourself."

I cried into the phone while she just sat there, saying, "There, there."

Once I finally caught my breath, Grammy continued. "You know, I have a picture you sent of Bernie on my refrigerator. He had such a cute little smile."

I nodded, and I smiled, remembering it.

She cleared her throat. "Lily must be sad, too."

I held my breath. "She doesn't know. Um. We're not speaking."

"Oh? She didn't tell me. I'm sorry to hear that. You know, this might be a good time to make up—you could really use her support right now."

"No, she has a new best friend, who she told all of my secrets to—our recipes and other stuff," I said.

"Lily did that? Hmm . . . that doesn't sound like her. Did you *hear* her tell this girl your secrets?"

"No, but she told her that I won't eat red foods, and they were laughing the other day. Probably about me eating my candy bars with a fork and a knife. So I can't tell her about what happened with Bernie."

"Fair enough. Then you be sure to let your parents know if you need to talk some more. Or give me a call. I'm always here—except for Sunday nights when I play bingo."

"Thanks, Grammy."

"You know, an Eskimo legend says that stars may actually be openings in Heaven. They say that our lost ones' love shines down on us to let us know they're happy. And Ana?" She paused. "You made your guinea pig very happy. I'll bet you'll see a really bright star tonight."

I smiled.

That night I made Bernie's favorite Strawberry, Grape, and Green Pepper Fruit Kabobs. Mom, Dad, and I went out on the patio and ate them where Bernie could shine down on us.

Chapter 12

I hardly slept that night, and the first thing I did in the morning was roll over to tell Bernie about it. That's when I remembered that he was the reason I was so sad.

I dragged myself to the bathroom to shower, but as the water ran over me, I just couldn't feel clean. *Lily, Explorations, Bernie, Bernie, Bernie.* The thoughts kept tumbling around in my head.

"You okay in there?" Mom asked, knocking on the bathroom door.

"Almost done," I said. But I kept washing. *Lily, Explorations, Bernie.*

As I lathered, the bar of soap got smaller and smaller until it was nothing but a nub. That was how my heart felt—like soon there'd be nothing left.

"Ana?" Dad called to me from the hall.

"I'm showering."

"You need to finish and get to school."

"I will."

Lather, lather, rinse. Lather, lather, rinse.

I could tell Dad was still standing outside the bathroom door, waiting.

Finally, I shut off the water and threw out what was left of the soap.

I ended up running all the way to school and barely making it into class before the bell rang.

"Wow, you were almost late!" Dasher joked as I sat down in the seat next to hers.

I shrugged.

"Wanna help me after school today? I think I can beat my old time for getting the dropped dog in the sled bag."

I shook my head. There was no way I could open my mouth to speak without bawling like a baby.

"Really? You always want to help out. Well, do you want *me* to come over to work on our recipes, then? I have an idea for a Hawaiian pancake. It'd be like Hawaiian pizza with pineapple and ham on it. Oh, or, I know! Pineapple syrup. Whaddya think? Wanna try it?"

I shook my head again.

"You okay?"

I nodded, and she finally left me alone.

The more I thought about it, the more I wondered if Bernie had gotten sick because of me. I was exposed to microorganisms all day at school, and he was only ever around me and my parents. I probably had cold germs on me from my unclean school, and I passed them on to him when I petted him. How could I have been so careless?

At lunch, I squirted antibacterial lotion on my hands and rubbed them together while I sang the alphabet song in my head (in English and then in French), making sure to sanitize every square inch of skin.

"You sure you're okay, Ana?" Dasher asked, watching my hands go round and round each other as she sat down.

"Just fine," I lied.

All day I felt like germs were haunting me, glowing on everything around me. *When was my chair last cleaned? Who sat in it before me? Did anyone touch the dial on my locker?*

As my social studies teacher, Miss Ross, took attendance, I started to worry about my clothes touching the back of the chair. I scooted my chair out and sat on the very edge of it so that only a small section of my jeans was exposed to the seat. I'd throw them right in the wash when I got home.

And then it hit me: if Bernie could get sick, so could Sweet Pea. *She could be sick right now!*

"All right. Clear your desks," Miss Ross said, setting a test in front of each of us.

I had forgotten that today was the big Ancient Civilizations test.

I looked at the first problem:

The Mayans lived in the area that is now _____.
A. California B. China C. Mexico D. Syria

Simple: C. I was about to fill in the bubble when Miss Ross COUGHED into her hand—the same hand she had used to pass out the tests!

I tried to fill in the bubble for C without holding my paper. It wasn't easy. I colored way outside the lines.

Did I already touch the paper? I wondered. *Should I go wash my hands?* I would definitely need to throw out the pencil I was using, since the tip was touching the paper. I didn't want Sweet Pea to get Miss Ross's disease.

"Ana, is everything all right?" Miss Ross whispered to me. "You don't have much time left, and you're only on number two."

"I'm okay," I said, looking down at my test.

All right, question number two . . .

The Mayans grew which of the following?
A. Beans B. Chili Peppers C. Maize D. Squash
E. All of the Above

A. I began filling it in, but then realized the answer was E: all of the above.

There was no way to erase what I'd filled in without holding on to the paper. I had to stay healthy so Sweet Pea wouldn't get sick. I'd just have to get that question wrong.

Could the cough germs on the paper radiate off of it—like those perfume samples in magazines? While I answered question three, I tried not to breathe in, which was impossible. I finally held my breath as long as I could, and then turned to the side to suck in fresh air.

Back to question three—

The bell rang.

"Okay, class, put your tests on my desk on your way out the door," Miss Ross said. "See you tomorrow."

No way was I touching that test. I snuck out of the classroom, leaving mine on my desk and not caring whether it got graded or not.

The minute I got home from school, I started washing. And washing. I felt completely covered in contaminants.

I rinsed my hands, soaped them up, lathered, rinsed them again, and dried them off, only to do it all over again. All that work with Dr. Taylor, down the drain. Literally. Luckily, Mom and Dad weren't home to see me and start worrying once again.

I got out a fresh towel and hid the sopping wet one in my closet.

When I finally pulled myself together, I biked over to the Hopkinses'. I didn't feel like telling Dasher I was there, so I went right into the dog pen.

I sat on the cold ground next to Sweet Pea's doghouse.

"Sweet Pea, something horrible happened."

I told her about Bernie. Sweet Pea took a couple steps out of her doghouse, and looked up at me with her sad chocolate eyes.

"He was the best guinea pig that ever lived, Sweet Pea."

Sweet Pea licked my hand and laid her head in my lap. I let my hands rest in her thick fur, and we stayed that way a long time.

Chapter 13

"Ana, ready to go?" Mom called from outside my bedroom door.

"Almost."

It was the night of the Halloween party, and Dasher had somehow convinced me to go with her. "I don't really want to go by myself," she had said at lunch, "but I don't know anyone else that well. Please?"

I promised her I'd go. Just for a little while.

I had made a costume at the last minute since I couldn't go as just a salt shaker with no pepper. I had painted a large rectangular box yellow, covered it in waxed paper, and pasted the word BUTTER on the side. I wished Bernie could have seen it—he always loved my costumes. He loved the holiday, too—eating the pumpkin chunks from our jack-o-lanterns and letting Lily and me dress him up in goofy costumes.

As I walked out of my room, carrying my butter costume, I caught sight of my reflection in the mirror—my face wore a permanent frown. It was the end of October, and Lily and I still hadn't made up. She had probably planned a matching costume with Via this year, instead of me—especially since they were cooking buddies. I assumed by now Via knew every cooking trick I had ever invented.

I gasped, thinking about it. She had probably also noticed all of my germ-prevention tips in my recipes. I bet she and Lily sat around looking at them and laughing.

Would they be at the party?

At least I wasn't going alone. I could at least look like I had a friend, too.

As Mom drove me to school, I realized I was making A's into my hand. I hoped going to the party would help keep my mind off of Bernie and Lily for a little while—but I didn't know if that was possible.

When we got to school, Dasher was standing outside, waiting for me.

"You came!" she said, running over to the car while Mom got my costume out of the trunk.

I carefully pulled the box over my head.

"Awesome costume," she said. "A stick of butter—that's so funny!"

"Why aren't you wearing one?" I asked. She had on her usual snow boots, scarf, and hat.

"I am. I'm a musher. Ready to go in?"

"I'll pick you up at seven, okay?" Mom asked. That was code for "That's three hours from now; will you be all right?" I hadn't brought my phone since I didn't have any pockets.

Dasher was looking at me like she knew I wanted to just crawl back into the car and go home. Her eyes pleaded for me to stay.

I nodded at Mom—my code for "Yeah, I'll survive."

Dasher and I walked into the gym to booming Halloween music. All the girls were standing in a clump near the DJ, and the boys were filling plates with candy and cookies.

I looked around for Lily, but the coast was clear.

"Hey, check it out." Dasher pointed to a sign that read GAMES IN THE ART ROOM. "Wanna go watch?"

We went into the art room, where the eighth-grade class president, Jessica O'Brien, was explaining the rules. "The first game is bobbing for apples. Whoever gets the most wins a prize."

I could tell her who was gonna get the least: me. I'd never put my mouth on food other kids had touched.

"Who wants to go first?"

"I will," Dasher volunteered.

She clasped her hands behind her back.

"One, two, three!" Jessica counted.

Everyone watched as Dasher stuck her face into the vat of water on top of the art table. Her teeth scraped an apple, and it bounced out of her mouth's reach.

"Aw," the crowd said, like we were at the final hole of a golf tournament.

Two more apples grazed her mouth and bobbed to the other side of the container. Then, *crunch!* Dasher lifted her head, an apple in her mouth like she was a roasted pig at a luau. She set the apple on the table and stuck her face back in the water to try again. I shivered. I wouldn't be eating apples any time soon; that was for sure.

"Time's up!" Jessica said. "Who's next?" She looked over at me, but when I shook my head she moved onto somebody else.

I wished I had my hand sanitizer with me, but there wasn't anywhere to store it in my butter costume.

"Hi, Ana."

I turned around to see Lily standing behind me, dressed as a chef. Of course, her new best friend Via was there, too. At least Via was dressed as a rock star—they hadn't come as twins. Via was busy talking to a zombie-princess and laughing her head off. Probably telling the girl all about my OCD.

"I . . . like your costume," Lily said to me.

I nodded, but I couldn't get any words to come out.

She twirled her finger around her hair. "I wanted to tell you—"

"Me and Ana can go first!" Dasher said suddenly, coming from behind me and pulling on my arm.

"What?" I turned around to see Dasher talking to Tasha, who was in my PE class.

"They're doing a haunted-kitchen thing in the supply closet," Dasher said. "It sounds like fun. You wanna try it?"

Everyone looked at us, including Lily and Via. I definitely couldn't back down now. I felt so hot in my costume—more like melted butter than a stick of it. But I could do this. "All right," I said.

Dasher and I followed Tasha over to the closet.

"Here, let me tie blindfolds on you two," she said, and put one on Dasher and then one on me. "There." She cleared her throat and cackled like a witch. "Welcome to my dungeon."

I rolled my eyes beneath the blindfold.

Tasha opened the door and led us inside the art supply closet.

"First, feel the brains I've collected." She took my hands and stuffed them into a large bowl. Without even needing to move my fingers around, I could tell the "brains" were actually overcooked pasta noodles—elbow macaroni, to be exact.

Dasher laughed. "Yuck!"

I wiped my hands off on my shorts. I was glad no one had played the game before us.

"Now, here are eyeballs I use in my stews." It was hard to tell from feeling them what the eyeballs really were, but they smelled a lot like grapes. I couldn't help thinking of Bernie, and how juice would dribble down his furry chin when he ate them . . .

"Ewww, that feels gross," Dasher said.

Bernie... I thought. I missed him so much.

"And last," Tasha said, taking my hands, "is the *blood*—"

My hands were suddenly being dunked into something warm and thick. It was blood! My hands were in a bucket of real blood!

I screamed, pulling my hands out and frantically sliding my fingers on my arms to get it off. Real blood! They'd used real blood!

I yanked off my blindfold and looked down.

In front of me were bottles of corn syrup right next to a big bucket of it. It wasn't even colored red.

The art teacher, Mrs. Choi, came running in and turned on the light. "What's wrong, honey? Are you all right?" She put her hands on my shoulders. "It was just warm corn syrup. It's not real blood." She squeezed gently. "You're okay, you're okay."

But I wasn't. I felt contaminated. *Majorly* contaminated.

I ran out of the supply closet and through the art room, where everyone, including Lily and Via, looked up to see what had happened. I kept running, right down the hallway and into the bathroom.

A bowl of blood, a bowl of blood. What an awful, awful image.

I started crying. I could feel myself getting sweaty and panicky and—oh, this was just too much! My hands needed to be washed ASAP.

I knew I should take my costume off while I washed, but I didn't want my dirty hands to touch it. Instead, I thrust my hands into the sink, letting the water splash across the front of it, getting the paper all wet.

That's when I heard someone outside, and I hurried into one of the stalls.

The bathroom door opened and closed, and there was a knock on my stall. "Ana? It's me—Dasher. What happened?"

"Nothing. I just feel really sick."

"Sorry for making you do the game. Is that why you're sick?"

"No, no. It's something I ate. Just go back to the art room. Please. I'm fine."

"You're not mad at me, are you?" she asked.

"No. I'll talk to you later."

Dasher stood outside the stall for another minute, then finally turned and left. When she was gone, I let myself out and grabbed paper towel after paper towel from the dispenser, setting them next to the sink. I knew I'd be there for a while. I washed and washed, ignoring the other girls that came in and saw me there.

Rinse, soap, rinse. Rinse, soap, rinse.

I couldn't stop thinking about it. *You put your hands in blood,* my brain said.

No, I didn't! I thought back. But I couldn't get the thoughts out of my head!

Breathe, Ana. And count down from twenty, I told myself.

The bathroom door opened again, and I saw Lily in the mirror.

"Omigod, Ana, are you okay?"

I finished counting down. Closed my eyes and opened them again.

"No, I'm not. Where's your new BFF?" I asked sarcastically. "Did she enjoy watching me freak out?"

"If you're talking about Via, she's in the art room," Lily said. "But let's drop it."

She slid the ponytail holder out of her hair and used it to pull my hair out of my face. "What happened?"

I told her about the game with the bowl of blood. I knew it sounded stupid to react that way to corn syrup, but Lily didn't laugh.

"Oh no!" she said. "Okay. We can handle this . . ." She dabbed at the water on my butter box with a paper towel. "What did Dr. Taylor tell you to do when stuff like this happens?"

Just then, Dasher came back into the bathroom. "Hey, Ana. I told Mrs. Choi you're sick, and she made me call your mom. She's on her way. Want me to watch for her?"

I nodded, and Dasher closed the bathroom door.

"Lily," I said. "How am I going to get from here to the car? Everyone will look at me. They'll probably talk about it for the rest of the school year—no, until I graduate high school . . ."

"No, they won't. I won't let them." She put her arm around me and helped me out the door. "Come on."

Lily led me through the hallway, explaining "She doesn't feel well," as people stared at my torn and dripping wet costume. She didn't slow down once—just kept guiding me toward the front door.

Dasher met us by the door. "Your mom's here."

Lily nodded and kept walking me toward the door.

"I hope you feel better!" Dasher shouted after us.

Then Lily and I were outside, and Mom was right there.

"Oh, honey, your costume!" She pulled it off over my head like I was a two-year-old, while I just stood there.

"Go ahead and get in the car, Ana," Mom said. "I just need to talk to Lily for a second."

Feeling defeated, I climbed into the passenger seat.

Once she finished getting the lowdown of the party-gone-wrong from Lily, Mom drove me home.

At a stoplight, she pointed to a star. "I believe that's Mars," she said and smiled. "Seeing things like that reminds me how big the universe is, and how each moment in our life is so small." She glanced over at me. "You're gonna get through this, Ana."

She patted my leg until the light turned green.

ANA'S BREAKFAST TRIFLE

$\frac{1}{2}$ cup cornflakes
1 small banana, sliced
1 tbsp raisins
1 small container vanilla yogurt
$\frac{1}{2}$ cup granola
1 tbsp chocolate chips (optional)

1. Wash hands thoroughly. Sanitize countertop. Examine utensils; if they appear dirty, find cleaner ones.
2. Find a medium-sized, clear bowl. Wash and dry.
3. Pour cornflakes into bowl, and shake the bowl gently until they form an even layer.
4. Cover with banana slices, and then spoon raisins on top. If you touch the banana or raisins, throw out.
5. Spoon yogurt on top.
6. Shake granola over mixture.
7. Top with chocolate chips.
8. Eat slowly, since you have nothing better to do.

Chapter 14

I carried my trifle to the kitchen table. Thank God it was Saturday, and I wouldn't have to face Lily, Via, or Dasher until Monday. I wished I never had to go back to school.

"Morning, sweetie," Mom said, kissing the top of my head. "Did you sleep okay last night?"

"I guess." I avoided eye contact and waited for it.

"So . . . the party last night . . ."

There it was.

"I know what you're thinking—I went overboard with my hand washing again," I said, picking up a chocolate chip with my spoon. "But, Mom, anyone would've freaked out thinking their hand was in a bowl of blood."

"I agree. But I'm more concerned that I woke up and heard you in the bathroom washing your hands for twenty minutes at midnight, and again at two in the morning."

I hadn't known she'd been able to hear me. I had only turned the faucet on halfway so it wouldn't be as loud.

"And Friday while you were at the party, Miss Ross called saying you failed your social studies test. She said you only answered two of the questions. And you haven't been turning in your homework. Is this because of Bernie? Or related to your OCD?" she asked.

I shrugged and swirled my spoon around in my uneaten trifle.

"I think we need to see—"

"No, Mom!" I threw down my spoon. "She'll make me do weird stuff again. Like touch real blood or something!"

"Honey, Dr. Taylor is there to help you. I know some of your therapy seems . . . strange . . . to you, but you've made real progress with her."

"But I'm fine now—I haven't been washing my hands that much. Just after the Halloween party, that's all."

She put her hands on her hips. "Let me see them."

"Okay, but remember that winter's coming up, and the cold weather dries out everybody's skin . . ." I said.

She ran her fingers over my hands and sighed. "I'm going to set up an appointment for next week."

"Mom," I whined.

But then the doorbell rang.

Oh, no. What if it was Dasher? She thought I was sick.

"Mom, I'm not here—or, I'm in bed. Please!" I ran to my room and closed the door.

But a couple minutes later, there was a knock on my bedroom door.

"Ana, it's me—Lily."

Lily?! I jumped off the bed and ran over to the door. Before I opened it, I paused. Was I still supposed to be angry with her? Should I thank her for helping me at the party?

I'm as cool as a cucumber, I told myself. I smoothed down my shirt and straightened my posture before opening the door.

"Hi." The way she said it was like old times, and I felt my shoulders relax. This was Lily, not some stranger. "You okay?"

I nodded. "Come in." I closed the door behind her.

Lily looked around my room. "Where's Bernie Toast?"

I gulped. I had forgotten that she didn't know.

I flopped onto my bed. "Bernie . . . passed away."

She plopped down next to me. "What? When?"

"A couple weeks ago."

"No!" she said and stuck out her bottom lip like she was trying to keep from crying. "Why didn't you call me?"

I looked down.

"Look, I know you're super mad at me," Lily said. "But I want to explain about Explorations."

I played with a loose thread on my comforter.

"Via knew how much I liked to bake, and she wanted to bake, too," Lily said. "But I would *never* share our recipes with someone else. So we thought about what else we could do for our project. Via really wanted to make money somehow, so we decided to start a catering business." She lay back and stuffed a pillow under her head. "We're going to have a couple menu items, and we'll serve food when our moms have book club meetings and stuff."

Wow. That was such a great idea. Why hadn't I thought of it?

"So anyway, Via and I are going to just make easy desserts and appetizers. But nothing from our cookbook. I swear!"

"So you never shared our recipes with her?"

"Not even 'Stir-Fried Pickles,'" she said. That was the first recipe in our Disasters: Deadly Combinations section.

"Why didn't you just tell me that?" I asked. "We could've ended this fight weeks ago."

"You wouldn't listen. You can be so stubborn and jealous . . ." Her eyes flicked to my hand, where I was making A's, and she stopped herself. "But you're my best friend. I should've tried harder."

I nodded. "I guess you're right—I *can* be stubborn some-times. Okay, so I was also jealous that you and Via were partners *and* were getting to cook. And that she's normal."

"Whoa. First of all, you're normal. Just . . . quirky. And second, just because I'm friends with Via doesn't mean *we* can't still be friends," she said. "People can have more than one friend."

"I know, but I don't want to be friends with anyone else. You're the only one that understands me."

"How do you know?" Lily asked, twirling a strand of her hair around her finger.

"Because I've seen other girls look at me washing my hands in the bathroom—they think I'm crazy."

"Who thinks that?" Lily said, sitting up.

I laughed. "It's okay. I don't blame them. Anyway, just drop it. As long as we're friends, I'm good."

"So . . . truce?" she asked.

"Truce."

I breathed a sigh of relief, and she did the same. Then I remembered what happened with Via.

"Via knows about my OCD, doesn't she?"

"I don't think so," Lily said. "I never said anything to her about it."

"But she made fun of me washing my hands so much, and how I ordered my lunch."

"No, no, no. That's just Via. She doesn't mean any harm by it. Really."

I wasn't so sure, but I still felt like a huge weight had been lifted off my shoulders. Lily and I were friends again. And she'd stand up for me—maybe even against Via.

"Come with me to the kitchen," I said. "I made something new."

I put together a fresh breakfast trifle for her, and we went back to my room.

"So," I started, cutting through my trifle with a spoon, "did you guys create a menu yet?"

"Um. Yeah. You know how Via mentioned at lunch that her mom doesn't really cook?" Lily asked. "Well, she wasn't kidding. First of all, on Saturday, I went to her house to create an appetizer recipe, and her fridge had, like, a jar of salsa, some pickles, and an old cream cheese sample."

I laughed. "You could've made a dip for the pickles by mixing the salsa and cream cheese."

"Ugh, I *so* wish you could work with us! You're a food genius! But anyway, that was only half of it. So we biked over to my house, and I thought we could make a spicy dip, so I put her in charge of the hot sauce. Well, I told her to put in a dash . . ."

I grimaced, knowing where her story was headed.

"Anyways," she continued. "I guess we'll stick to things like brownies and PB&J or something."

I nodded and told her all about Dasher and the smoke detector.

"Oh boy," she said. "What are we going to do? And your pancake recipes sound fab—I want to add them to my binder."

My phone pinged; it was Dasher.

Do you feel better? I'm practicing for the race. Want to come over?

Last time she saw me, I was sopping wet and freaking out. I really didn't want to lie to her, but there was no way I could explain my situation.

I looked over at Lily, who was flipping through my recipe binder, a look of awe on her face.

I swallowed. No, I can't. I'm still sick, I texted back.

That stinks. What do you have?

The flu.

The barfing kind?

yes, I typed in lowercase, like that would somehow make my lie less awful.

Let me know if you feel better tomorrow. I think I came up with a new pancake recipe we can try.

I'll call you if I do. Say hi to Sweet Pea for me. I clicked off my phone.

I felt bad for ditching Dasher, but what was I supposed to do? I had been in Lily withdrawal for weeks.

"Was that Dasher?" Lily asked. "Does she know about your OCD and stuff?"

"No! She's just my partner for Explorations," I said. "So, wanna try a recipe for a breakfast cookie?"

"Sure." She jumped off my bed, and we headed to the kitchen.

"Hey, now I can sit with you at lunch again!" I squealed.

"I missed you, Analily!" Lily said.

"I missed you, too, Liliana."

I smiled—my first real smile in a long time.

Chapter 15

I didn't go to Dasher's over the weekend. I felt bad, but Lily and I were just super busy baking together. We tried out a bunch of new recipes that were too complicated to do with Dasher or Via, like banana-cinnamon rolls and orange-turkey frittata.

But at least I had made Dasher a special treat on Sunday night: Musher Mix, an assortment of chunky cereals, pretzels, M&Ms, and dried mango pieces.

I hid the bag and a copy of the recipe behind my back as I walked into class. I thought the recipe was a great one because it was so simple she could make it on her own, too.

After a little while the bell rang. But Dasher never showed up.

At lunch I sat at my old table with Lily (and Via). I kept looking over at Dasher's table to see if she had come to school late, but her spot stayed empty.

"What did Dasher think of the mix you made her?" Lily asked, spooning some of her Pork-and-Bean Dip onto a water cracker.

"She's not here today."

"Is she sick?"

I shrugged. "I don't know."

"Didn't you have the flu at the Halloween party?" Via asked. "She must've caught it from—"

"Was she sick this weekend?" Lily interrupted.

I shrugged again. "I don't know. I didn't see her." I hoped nothing had happened to her. What if her rig tipped over deep in the woods somewhere, leaving her hanging off a cliff—not that we lived anywhere near a cliff. I began drawing A's in my hand.

Lily smacked at it. "She's fine. It's probably the flu." She glanced sideways at me and quickly continued, "Or something not contagious. Eat your lunch."

And then it hit me: that's how Bernie died—while I was at school. I sucked in a deep breath and then tried yoga-breathing to calm myself down.

"Don't think about it," Lily said quietly.

"Don't think about what?" Via asked.

I plastered a smile on my face. Three more hours before I could check on Dasher. "Nothing."

After school, I pretty much ran all the way home. I tried texting Dasher, but she never texted back. I knew it: she was hanging over the edge of a cliff.

"Bye, Mom. I'm riding over to Dasher's," I said, grabbing the trail mix to give her. If something had happened, she was probably hungry—maybe even malnourished.

As I rode, I realized that Dasher might actually be sick with the flu. I slowed a little.

Ana, it's not the end of the world if you get the flu, I told myself. *You've already been exposed, anyway.*

I checked my throat glands as I rode.

Once I got to Dasher's, it didn't take long to figure out what was wrong with her. She was out by the dog pens—hopping around on crutches.

"What happened?" I asked.

Cubby dumped some food into one of the dog's food bowls. "She fell."

"Off the sled?"

"No," Dasher said. "Baking."

"Baking? How did you fall . . . baking?"

"Yesterday I decided to try the new recipe I made up—chocolate pancakes," she explained. "So, first, I made a batch, and they were super salty. It turned out I used salt instead of sugar. So I had to make another batch." She shifted on her crutches.

"It called for two eggs, so I tried to crack them together—kind of like a fancy chef might do. Well, I forgot to do it over the bowl, and most of the egg fell on the ground. I decided to clean up later since I'd probably get other stuff on the floor anyway." Dasher bent over as best as she could to rub one of the dogs' ears.

"So I ate my pancakes—which tasted awful by the way—and then, *bam*. I slipped on the egg on the floor and landed on my foot funny."

"She has a strained ankle," Cubby said.

"Sprained," Dasher corrected him. "Well, we don't know what's wrong with it, but it's all swollen."

"Wow," I said. "Does it hurt a lot?"

"It did. Dad said I'm supposed to stay off it, but I gotta feed the dogs, clean up after 'em . . . everything. They'd know something was up if I didn't."

"What about getting ready for the race?" I asked.

"If the swelling doesn't go away, Mom's taking me to the doctor's for x-rays and stuff."

I felt horrible. If I had been here, none of this would've happened—there's no way I would've left egg on the floor.

"I made you a treat," I said and handed her the Musher Mix. "It's for when you're out on the trail. Well, it was . . ."

"Thanks. You've been so nice to me," Dasher said.

That made me feel even worse.

"Um . . . so, how was the rest of the party?" I asked.

"After you left, I called my mom to pick me up."

"Oh. I'm sorry I ruined it for you," I said.

"It's okay. When I got home, I went trick-or-treating with Cubby. It was so awesome! Back in Alaska, my mom had to drive us house to house, and we hardly got anything. But here, houses are so close together. Mom dropped us off in town, and we filled our bags in, like, a half hour!" She reached into her jeans pocket and pulled out a mini box of Milk Duds and some gumballs that looked like eyeballs. "Want some?"

Just the thought of gum made me gag (all those germs being chewed and rechewed), so I took the box of Milk Duds.

"Thanks. Want help feeding the dogs?" I asked.

"Sure."

"We'll feed the females first," Cubby ordered me.

I helped Cubby fill their food bowls while Dasher sat on a lawn chair with her leg propped up on a big bag of dog food.

"It's been days since they've gotten good exercise," Dasher said. "Ghost is going stir-crazy."

"Cubby and I can walk them," I said.

"Cool," Dasher said. "But first I have to finish my homework. And Cubby, Mom said you have to practice for your recital. Ana, you can hang out here if you want."

I nodded and, after she and Cubby went inside, I let myself into the female pen to walk Sweet Pea.

"Sweet Pea, are you a sled dog?" I asked.

Her tail wagged.

"I knew you were. Let's try something . . ."

I had seen Dasher train puppies with an old tire attached to a leash. Why couldn't Sweet Pea do that?

Sweet Pea stood still as I got the leash and tire from the barn and attached her harness to them. Then I walked next to her, afraid it might be too heavy after all, but she loved it! She pulled with such determination. When I went to take the tire off, she looked up at me with her goofy dog grin like she wanted to try it again.

"Well, I guess you answered my question," I said, rubbing her behind her ears.

Since it was dark out by the time we finished, Mom came to pick me up. We put my bike in the trunk.

On the way home, I told her about Dasher's ankle.

"How awful for her! Who would have thought baking was so dangerous?" she joked.

"There're lots of ways—"

"Yes, yes, I know." She turned down the radio and cleared her throat. "So, I made you an appointment with Dr. Taylor. For tomorrow afternoon."

"Mom! Do I have to? The last couple days I've gotten much better. Really." And I totally had.

"Even so, I think it's good to touch base with her."

I looked out the car window. Maybe if *I* slipped on an egg, I'd get out of going.

Chapter 16

I carried the overflowing pot of popcorn from the stovetop over to the table and poured it into two bowls—one for me and one for Dad (Mom preferred my raisin caramel corn).

Grammy's Old-Fashioned Popcorn hit the spot whenever I was nervous about something. It always made me think of her, and what she would say or do to make me feel better.

Every summer, Lily and I visited her lake house in Michigan. Normally I loved going there, but the summer before fourth grade, I couldn't even bring myself to put my toes in the water.

"What's wrong, Ana?" Grammy had asked, and I told her how I thought the lake water could be contaminated and that I didn't want to go in it. She had nodded and said, "Come join me in the kitchen, and help me make popcorn."

Grammy had poured oil into her copper-bottomed pot and swirled it around while I went to the cabinet to get the old coffee tin filled with popcorn kernels. Grammy took two kernels and threw them in the pot, where they exploded, showing us that the oil was ready.

I scooped up kernels with her dented, metal measuring cup, and she dumped them into the pot. "Do you miss swimming?" she asked.

I hurried to cover the pot with a lid. "Yeah, I guess. I was fine last summer."

"Sometimes our brains put thoughts into our heads—silly thoughts that we start to believe." She cut off half a stick of butter and dropped it into a second pot. "And sometimes you just have to take the risk and hope that those thoughts are wrong."

"But what if they aren't wrong? What if I do get sick from the water?"

"There are risks involved with a lot of things in life. But we can't avoid everything—or we wouldn't be living, would we?"

I poured the butter onto the popcorn. "So you think I should go in the lake?"

"You need to decide that for yourself." She had smiled and sprinkled Parmesan cheese on top of the mix. And then she said, "You know what? I'm going in—it's hot in here! Our popcorn will make a good after-swimming snack." She patted my hand and left to put on her swimsuit.

After munching on a few pieces of popcorn, I marched back to the lake. Lily and the other kids were still there. I sat down on the dock and slowly stuck my toes in the water. *I'll just sit here for a minute and then wash them off under the hose*, I told myself.

As I sat there, we all started chatting. Next thing I knew, my feet were in the water.

By the end of that summer, I was splashing around as much as Lily.

That had been two years ago, but making Grammy's popcorn still helped me remember that I needed to face my fears or risk missing out on something, like swimming in the lake.

Grammy always said my therapy visits were to "freshen up" on what Dr. Taylor taught me, just like she did with her lipstick after dinner. If only it were that easy.

As I sat on the couch, munching my worries away in front of the TV, Dad came in.

"Hi, Gourmet Pumpkin. You ready for your appointment tomorrow?" he asked.

"Not really."

He picked up his bowl of popcorn and joined me on the couch. "I know you don't want to go, but your OCD is affecting school again."

I drew A's on the side of my popcorn bowl. "Do you think I'll ever be normal?" I asked.

Dad popped a couple pieces of popcorn in his mouth. "Ana, try to remember that those thoughts aren't really yours—they're just your OCD trying to make you do things you don't need to. When you're already upset about something, like Bernie Toast, your OCD knows you're vulnerable and puts bad, unwanted thoughts in your head. Going to Dr. Taylor will help get you back on track."

Dad shoved another handful of popcorn into his mouth and shook his head. "I never want you to think you're not normal because of this. You're more than normal—you're a smart, funny, and compassionate person. And"—he threw a piece of popcorn in the air and caught it in his mouth—"you're one heck of a chef."

"What happened to Dasher?" Lily asked when I met her in the lunch line the next day. "I saw her on crutches." She selected a plate of spaghetti with no red sauce. "Can I have, like, six things of butter?" she asked the lunch lady.

I grabbed a milk, telling Lily all about Dasher's cooking incident.

"I thought that stuff only happened in cartoons," she said. I followed her to our old table and sat down. Luckily, Via wasn't there yet—I had Lily all to myself.

As I sanitized my hands, I noticed Dasher sitting at the table we'd shared for the last couple of months. She was looking around.

Then she spotted me. I waved from my table, but she looked confused.

Oh. The day before I had sat with Lily, but Dasher hadn't been around to notice.

I bit my lip. I guessed I should've told Dasher I couldn't sit with her anymore.

"I'll be right back," I told Lily.

I knew the right thing to do was ask Dasher to join us. But Lily and I still had a lot of catching up to do, and I really just wanted it to be her and me. I knew Dasher would want to talk about the race, and then Lily would feel left out.

"Hi, Dasher," I said as I walked up to her table.

"Hey—you're late to lunch."

"Sorry, I can't sit with you. I'm . . . helping Lily with her math."

"At lunch?"

I nodded, hoping my nose wasn't growing.

"Maybe you guys can sit here tomorrow, then?" she said.

"Um . . . the test is at the end of the week. We're kind of studying every day."

"That stinks. Well, do you wanna come over after school and help Cubby with the dogs?"

"Sure."

"Awesome."

I started to walk away.

"Hey," Dasher added. "Tell her good luck."

"Who?"

"Lily. On her test?"

"Oh. Yeah, thanks. I'll tell her." I walked back to my table. In my head, I could hear Mom *tsk*-ing me for lying.

During lunch, Via blabbed on and on, debating what to wear for their first catering job. "Maybe short sleeves with a mini, or long sleeves and leggings . . ."

I looked over at Dasher, who was all alone, again.

I had thought sitting with Lily would make me feel better. But instead, I felt awful.

Chapter 17

"You're late," Mom said as I got in the car for my appointment.

For once, I wanted nothing more than to still be in social studies, learning about Mesopotamian government, but ERP torture with Dr. Taylor awaited.

"Didn't your teacher let you leave when the office called?" Mom asked.

I didn't answer. I knew she knew I had spent time washing before heading out to the car.

Not wanting to talk about anything, I turned up the radio.

When we pulled up at the office, Mom said, "I just need to stop by the ATM, and then I'll be in the waiting room."

With a sigh, I went inside and signed in.

Before I even sat down, the waiting-room door opened. "Hi, Ana," Dr. Taylor said with a smile. "Come on back."

Dr. Taylor was okay, I guess. The first time I met her, she didn't even try to shake my hand, like she knew some people thought it was gross.

She had the brightest, most pumpkin-colored hair I'd ever seen. It was long and curly, like Lily's. And she had told me the first time I met with her that when she was my age she used to wrap strands of it around her finger and pull them out. It's called trichotillomania. She couldn't help doing it, and back then she did it so much that she had bald patches.

She had to see a doctor, too, who helped her stop. And once she did, she vowed to always wear her hair long and flowing.

Her dress was also flowy and made her look like a forest fairy, which, for whatever reason, made me feel better than talking to someone in a white coat.

She and I made the long trek to her office, walking past paintings of various kinds of flowers on the walls.

Dr. Taylor closed her office door behind me, and I sat down on the wooden chair she put out just for me—I wasn't ready for the cloth kind everyone else used. "How's your cookbook going?" she asked.

I told her about the sled dog race and some of the pancake recipes I had come up with.

"You're so creative," she said. "And they sound delicious."

I nodded looking down at the toys strewn across the floor: blocks, dolls, puppets, and balls.

She took my file off her desk and sat down in a chair across from me. She quickly scanned the pages, and I wondered what they said. Ana Morgan—crazy girl who washes her hands a lot. Previous visit: treatment included forcing her to touch dirty doorknobs. Recently freaked out at a party while dressed as a stick of butter.

I made A's in my hand.

"I see you started middle school since I last saw you. That must be quite a change." She flipped to the next page, read it, and then put the folder down. "So, what brings you in today?"

I had been afraid she'd ask that. Should I tell her everything? Nothing?

Dr. Taylor sat there, smiling, which I knew she'd keep doing until I answered her question.

"Uh. I guess I'm washing my hands a lot again?"

She nodded like that was a good answer and waited for me to say more, but I didn't. I tried to make my hands look normal by clamping them together.

She scribbled away on her notepad. *Patient clammed up*, it probably said. "Any idea how many times a day?"

I shook my head.

"Has it been impacting your schoolwork or time with friends?"

"Well, I guess I've missed parts of class a couple of times because I was in the bathroom. And my hands hurt because they're chapped from washing." I looked down at them. "And at my school's Halloween party . . ." A tear slid down my cheek.

Dr. Taylor passed me a tissue. "I spent the whole time washing my hands in the bathroom, and my friend had to walk me out to my mom's car."

"What caused you to wash your hands at the party?"

I took a deep breath and told Dr. Taylor the whole story about Bernie dying, the bobbing for apples, and the bowls of brains, eyeballs, and blood. If she was shocked or disgusted by what I said, she hid it well.

"It turned out to just be warm corn syrup, but I freaked. I try not to wash so much, but it's really hard when I feel like I've been covered in contaminants. And sometimes I know I'm being ridiculous, but I have to wash anyways, just to be safe."

"That must be very frustrating, knowing it's your OCD talking but not being able to stop it," Dr. Taylor said, shaking her head knowingly. "Have you been doing your ERP therapy?"

I nodded. "I've been trying to not wash my hands as often. It's just been harder lately."

Dr. Taylor gave me an anxiety test to find out if I had gotten better or worse. She never bothered to tell me whether I passed or failed, but the fact that I was still seeing her gave me an idea of the answer.

She went back over exercises I should do when something happened that made me feel contaminated, like waiting ten minutes before washing my hands or only allowing myself to wash for three minutes.

"So I don't have to touch toilet water or anything?" I asked, relieved.

"I'm not done. There's more."

Of course there was. I squirmed in my chair.

"You've done an excellent job with touching surfaces, Ana. I'm so proud of you. You can keep working on that as needed, but we're going to add something new. I know how much you like to cook," she said and smiled. "And that you're helping with the sled dog race's breakfast, so I think it's important that you're able to cook without washing your hands so often. I'm going to have you make cookie dough and dip your finger in the batter."

No, no, no. "What do I do with the batter after that?" I asked.

"You bake it. And you share the cookies with your parents."

"So they get sick? No, I don't think that's a good idea."

"Why do you think they'll get sick?"

"From my germs? In the cookies? There's no way to clean off every last speck of bacteria from my fingers. Like from under my fingernails, or between my fingers . . ." I looked at my hands, imagining all the spots that I probably missed each time I washed.

"Okay," Dr. Taylor said, holding up her hand. She wore a silver ring on every finger. "I understand. So, for now, I just want you to write down everything you think could happen from sticking your finger in the batter."

I exhaled.

"Email it to me after you get home. If I approve, I'll have you read your list out loud five times each night, recording your anxiety rating after each reading. Then we'll talk again on Sunday. In the meantime, keep working on touching surfaces."

What I wouldn't give for a sprained ankle instead of a nagging OCD brain.

By the time I got home, the school day had ended. Mom told me to start writing up my script right away. I picked up my phone to call Lily for moral support, but then I put it back down.

Lily had been there when I first started seeing Dr. Taylor, and she'd helped me get through my very first ERP homework when I had to touch the floor and doorknobs. But I was sure she thought I was past that kind of stuff. Having to do it all over again might be too much for her.

And, now that she was also friends with Via—who was disorder-free—maybe Lily'd realize how annoying my therapy was. Or how nice it was to not have to cheer on someone for everyday tasks. I could just see Via asking her, "So you need to congratulate Ana for touching a light switch?"

It was hard enough almost losing Lily once. No sense in telling her I had ERP homework again.

I got on the computer to write the dreaded script.

Although writing down what I was feeling should have been easy, even *thinking* of putting my finger in batter made me sick to my stomach. "But I gotta do it," I told myself. *Here goes . . .*

> If I were to stick my finger in cookie batter, I would
> be exposing my parents to all sorts of germs.

Because the dough is sticky, any bacteria on my finger would come off in the batter. I would stir it around, contaminating the entire bowl of dough. Then it would bake in. Maybe that type of bacteria would be heat-activated and multiply over and over until a whole colony of bacteria lived in the dough. Then Mom and Dad would eat the cookies. They'd both get really sick. Dad would probably have to quit work. We'd have to move out of our house because we'd have no money. We would become homeless on the streets and, once winter hit, it would be so cold out that we'd all freeze to death. The End.

Yeah, Dr. Taylor, really healthy exercise. I emailed it to her almost as a joke, and she replied back before I even finished my online game.

Looks great, she had written. Go ahead and start reading it aloud five times a day.

Was she nuts?

I left to wash my hands and get a snack before reading the dreaded script. Why did she want me to get these thoughts stuck in my brain? That made no sense.

Maybe this was a test to see if I had good judgment. Maybe I was supposed to recognize that creating contaminated cookie dough was, in fact, dangerous. Maybe I was supposed to refuse the ERP therapy.

As I was about to read the script aloud, I noticed I had a new email. The subject line said, From Grammy in Michigan.

Grammy? I opened the email.

> Dear Ana,
>   My friend's son got me an internet connection for my computer. I now have electronic mail. I hope you don't mind that Lily gave me your electronic email name.
>   How are you doing?
> Love,
> Grammy

I emailed her back about my latest quest with ERP, then flipped to a game until I noticed a new email message.

> Dear Ana,
>   Who knows what that head-shrinker is thinking. It won't hurt to try it, right? Sometimes it's surprising what happens.
> Love,
> Grammy

I had been hoping Grammy would tell me it was stupid to read through my contamination script.

I sighed and closed my laptop. I really didn't want to read what I had written.

Then I got an idea. I printed my script and headed for the door. "Bye, Mom. I'm going to Dasher's."

"Did you do your ERP assignment?" she asked, dropping a teabag into a teapot.

"That's what I'm going to do." I didn't wait for her response.

I was happy Mrs. Hopkins's car wasn't in the driveway when I biked up to the house. It meant Dasher was still at the doctor's and I could hang out with Sweet Pea alone. There was no way I could read my script in front of actual people—and the Hopkinses didn't mind me being there when they weren't.

As I went into the dog pen, Sweet Pea did her happy bark. "Hey, girl," I said, rubbing the top of her head. "I need your help with an assignment."

I threw some straw down for the two of us to sit on, and we both snuggled in for the ridiculous task ahead of us. "Okay, here goes."

I read my passage about baking my germs into cookies and making my family sick and homeless. Sweet Pea didn't look the least bit horrified, even though I was.

I wrote down my anxiety score: seventy out of a hundred. "Sorry, but now I'm supposed to read it again," I said. Still no reaction from Sweet Pea. I still thought it was awful, but I had to admit it was less surprising—around a sixty. We read it again and again and again. Finally, I got down to a thirty.

"Wow, I hope I didn't scar you for life or something," I said when we were finished. I rubbed the top of her head.

As I was packing up, the Hopkinses' car pulled into the driveway. I folded up my script and stuck it in my pocket.

I waved to Dasher, and she hobbled over to me as Mrs. Hopkins and Cubby went into the house.

"Horrible news," Dasher said. Her face was all pink and puffy, like she'd been crying. "The doctor said I tore some tendons." She hiccuped a little and then continued. "It's worse than a sprain." She shook her head and her face scrunched up before she started bawling. "Icatdouhraaaace."

"What?" I asked, but she was crying too hard to repeat it. I gasped. "Did you say you can't do the race?"

She nodded. I put my hands over my mouth. "But you've been practicing for it since you moved here!"

That made her cry harder.

"What if you heal in record time?" I said, nodding with encouragement. "I can help you stay off your foot. And I have recipes with superfruits . . ."

She wiped her nose on her coat sleeve and sniffed. "Even if I got better in time for the race, I wouldn't be able to train the dogs last minute."

I sighed. "Yeah, I didn't think of that." And then it hit me. "What about our Explorations project?" Our project depended on her racing!

"I know. We can't have a project about pancake recipes. My mom said we should just tell Mr. Creed we have to switch topics."

"Switch topics?" No way would Mr. Creed accept an excuse. Even if we were trapped under an avalanche, he'd expect us to turn in our project without a speck of snow on it.

My brain and heart were racing as I tried to figure out what we could possibly do. "I understand why you can't go around to feed all the dogs or get them hooked up, but why can't you race? Don't you just stand on the runners and let the dogs pull?" I asked.

Dasher choked out a laugh. "Not exactly."

"So what do we do?" I asked.

"I don't know. I guess we need to start thinking of other projects or something. And we can try to talk to Mr. Creed tomorrow."

Great. Anxiety up to one hundred and three.

Chapter 18

The next morning, Dasher hobbled into class just as the last bell rang.

"Ms. Hopkins," Mr. Creed started in. "Because you are on crutches, I will let it slide that you were not in your seat when the bell rang. However, tomorrow you need to figure out a way to get here on time. I will not accept any more excuses."

My eyes met Dasher's, and I gulped. So much for talking to him about our project change.

As Mr. Creed wrote on the board, Dasher passed me a note. Don't say anything to Mr. C yet. Will explain after class.

Phew—she must have come up with something. I relaxed a little.

After English, I walked Dasher to her next class, carrying her books.

"So I have an idea for our project," she said as we walked into her Spanish classroom.

"Good, because I couldn't really think of anything." I handed Dasher her books. "What's your idea?"

"*You* run the do—"

"*Disculpen*, señoritas," Dasher's teacher said. "*La clase ya empezo.*"

I had no idea what the teacher said, but I had a feeling she told me to get going.

What had Dasher wanted to say? I run the what? She couldn't mean dogs. Maybe dough? Doughnuts? But she was definitely going to say the word *dogs*. This couldn't be good. I needed Lily.

At lunch, I drew A's into my hand until Lily showed up at the lunch table.

"We have a situation," I told her.

"No problem." Lily stuck her lunch bag under her arm and got out her hand sanitizer.

For once it wasn't a germ emergency. "No, not like that. We have to find Dasher."

We looked around the cafeteria. Lily pointed to the superlong Pizza Day line. "There she is!"

"There who is? What's going on?" Via asked, plopping her plate of pizza down on the table. "Ana, you look like you're gonna pee your pants."

"Something's up," Lily told her. She turned to me. *Need me alone?* her eyes asked.

"No, just . . . come on, guys."

We joined Dasher in the lunch line.

I introduced everyone to each other, and then Dasher and I filled Via and Lily in on our situation.

"So the perfect solution is for Ana to run the race instead," Dasher said, like it was nothing.

"Maybe you can explain the situation to Mr.—" Lily began.

"You've obviously never met Mr. Creed," Via said with a laugh.

For once, I agreed with her.

Lily unwrapped her blueberry-and-cream-cheese sandwich and began eating it in line. "You know what? I think you can do it, Ana. You can mush," she said.

"She wouldn't be doing a distance race. Just a sprint. Four miles or so," Dasher told her.

"Four miles—oh, that's nothing!" Via said, pulling a piece off Lily's sandwich and eating it.

"What? No, I can't!" I said. "No, no. We'll just . . . come up with a new project. Yeah. I can do most of the work if I stay up all night—"

"Look! There's Mr. Creed," Via said, pointing as he walked by on his way to the teacher's lounge. "Let's see what he says. Hey, Mr. Creed!"

"Via, no!" I hissed, but it was too late. He strode toward us with a newspaper under his arm and a mug in his hand.

"Ms. Kirkland. This had better be important, as you are interrupting my lunch time."

"Yes, sir," Via said. "Tell him, Ana."

My eyes went wide, and I made A's on my lunch bag, shaking my head and hoping the ground would just suck me in.

"Speak up, Ms. Morgan. And quickly, as my time is valuable."

I opened my mouth, but nothing came out. My throat felt like a piping bag jammed with too-thick frosting.

"It's our Explorations project," Dasher said, leaning on my shoulder like a crutch. "I'm supposed to mush in a sled dog race, but I can't because of my stupid ankle. Ana wondered—*we* wondered—if we could do a different topic."

Yikes—Contractions City.

"A different topic? The project is due in less than six weeks. Do you expect to complete a new project within that time frame, when other pupils have been working on their reports since September?"

"What else can we do?" I blurted out, shocking myself.

"Figure out a way to assemble something that shows you put time into this assignment. Now, if you do not mind, I am going to try to enjoy my coffee, which is probably cold by now." He walked away.

"Wow," Lily said, smiling at me. "Who gave you a cup of courage?"

"He just makes me so . . . angry. Of course I can do it. Wait, what am I saying? I don't know anything about mushing."

"Actually, you do," Dasher said, picking up a lunch tray and scooching over to the counter to get a slice of gross, floppy cafeteria pizza. "What do you say to get the dogs to turn right?" she asked.

"Well, that's easy—*gee*," I answered.

"What do you say to pass other teams?"

I thought a minute. "On by."

"And how do you help the dogs go around a tight corner?"

"Lean into the turn." Wow, I knew more than I thought I did.

"And," Via said, excited, "that means Dasher will cook the breakfast for the race."

Dasher and I looked at one another.

We had a lot of work ahead of us.

Luckily, Dasher said we had to wait until the weekend to begin my training because her mom was making her study for her science test the next day, and Cubby's birthday was Friday. That gave me time to let it sink in before actually doing it. I still went over to the Hopkinses' to read my script to Sweet Pea.

As I snuggled up next to her, I told her my latest news. "So, I might be racing for Dasher now. Can you believe it?" Sweet Pea licked her lips, and I scratched her behind her ears. "Maybe we can convince Dasher to let you be part of my team."

Sweet Pea wagged her tail.

"Okay, time for The Exciting Story of the Contaminated Cookie Dough. Ready? 'If I were to stick my finger in cookie batter, I would be exposing my parents . . .'"

It didn't shock me anymore to read about the germs in the batter, or how they would multiply in the oven and ultimately kill us. In a way, it almost sounded strange. I recited the script four more times, less fazed each time. I even tried saying it with a French accent and a Southern accent. Sweet Pea napped through the last reading.

I folded up the paper. "Sorry, I know this isn't fun. But I have to do it. I'll see if I can get something different for us to read, okay?"

That night, Dr. Taylor did her follow-up call.

"How is your script reading going?"

"I'm *so* ready to do something different," I told her. "I'm sick of it."

"What number are you at on your anxiety scale?"

"About a fourteen."

"Great! Then you're ready to actually try it. I want you to make the cookie dough and put your finger in it. Then, bake the cookies and feed them to your family. You should eat some, too. Are you ready to do it?"

Number on anxiety scale: one hundred.

Chapter 19

I walked home from school as slowly as I could the next day, knowing that I'd have to start my ERP torture once I got there.

Luckily, Mom wasn't home yet. Maybe she had to work late, and we wouldn't be able to do it after all. Could I possibly be that lucky?

I was washing my hands at the kitchen sink when she came in the door.

"I sure am in the mood for some cookies," she said, trying to sound cheerful.

I grunted back and continued applying coat number six of soap.

Mom walked over and turned the water off. "Ready to start baking?"

No.

"Let's see, what do we need?" Mom started getting out the bowls and measuring cups.

I softened the butter in the microwave while she measured out the two kinds of sugar. As the mixer whirred, I added in the vanilla. I did it quickly so Mom couldn't see my secret: I always doubled the amount.

"All right," Mom said. "You'll need to put your finger in the batter before we add the eggs, so I guess it's time."

Time to kill our family with finger contaminants? I thought.

"Are you *sure* you want me to do this?" I asked. She was more likely to back down than Dad was. Before I started seeing Dr. Taylor, Mom had let me wash my hands as much as I wanted. Dr. Taylor had to convince her that letting me "perform my compulsions" wasn't helpful to me. I could tell Mom still felt bad making me go through ERP stuff, so I gave her a sad face to guilt trip her.

"Nope, puppy-dog eyes aren't going to work this time. Remember your script. Do you still think what you wrote will happen if you stick your finger in this batter?"

It did sound pretty ridiculous: the germs from my fingers causing my whole family to become homeless and eventually freeze to death. "Well, parts of it could happen."

"It's okay. Your dad and I are willing to take that risk. Stick your finger in there."

"Can I go wash—"

"Nope. Go on. Do you want me to count to three?"

I nodded and clenched my fists.

"One, two . . . three!"

I barely stuck my finger in the batter, leaving a fingerprint on the surface.

"Really get it in there," Mom said.

Wincing, I pushed my finger in like I was planting a seed. Although I wanted to make my brain think of something else, Dr. Taylor said I should concentrate on the disgusting task I was doing. And it was gross. Any particles of school bacterium that I had missed when washing my finger or under my nail were now sitting in the batter.

I pulled my finger out. My anxiety level went up like that carnival game where you strike a platform with a hammer trying to hit the bell. I *definitely* hit the bell.

"Good!" Mom said too cheerfully. "Let's mix up the batter."

I shook my head. "You do it," I said, tears blurring my eyes as I wiped my finger off with a napkin.

"No, Ana, you can do this. You've come so far. Take some deep breaths."

I hadn't noticed I was breathing so hard. I concentrated on slowing it down.

I got my anxiety down to a sixty-five.

"We have to keep going. Ready?" Mom asked.

Finally, I was able to click on the mixer. The dough spun around and around, germs mixing in like another ingredient.

I wished germs could be seen with UV lights or something. Then I could pick out the contaminated bits in the batter with tweezers and throw them away.

Heat kills germs, anyway, the sensible side of my brain reassured me. *Any bacteria you mixed into the cookies will be killed in the oven.*

But, my OCD reminded me, *heat also helps things grow. Think about how plants are nurtured by the sun and how heat makes bread dough double in size.*

"I'll add the eggs," Mom said, snapping my brain out of its argument with itself.

She cracked the eggs into the bowl. I poured in the dry ingredients, including a tablespoon of malt powder I snuck in.

She stirred in the chocolate chips. "All set."

"Now can we throw out the batter? I'll make a batch of PB&J Cookies, just for you." They were her favorite.

"You know we need to follow through with this." Mom chewed on her lip and looked at me. "But maybe you're not ready? Do you want to go back to reading your script and try this in a week?"

Postponing the task would make me even more anxious. I sighed. "No, let's just finish this."

With two spoons each, we arranged the dough onto the baking sheet.

Once the cookies were in the oven, Mom set the timer for nine minutes. I considered changing it to twenty since Mom wouldn't eat burnt cookies, but I didn't.

We worked on getting the kitchen cleaned up.

"So, Dasher's ankle is pretty bad," I said. "I'm going to have to mush in the race."

Mom stopped wiping the counter and looked up. "Really? Do you know how to mush?"

"Dasher's going to train me. And I've watched her a lot."

"Is it safe?"

"I guess. I'll wear a helmet and stuff." But maybe Mom was right. Maybe it wasn't safe. Maybe I was in over my head. "Unless you don't want me to do it. You could write Mr. Creed a note forbidding me."

"Is that what you want me to do?"

Part of me would have loved it if she called the school and forced Mr. Creed to let us do a different project. SHE CAN'T MUSH—SHE HAS OCD, the note could say. But that sounded silly, even to me.

I sighed. "No, I'll do it."

Dad walked in the door then and kissed Mom on the cheek. "Mmmm, nothing better than Ana's Classified Recipe for Chocolate Chip Cookies."

Yeah, nothing better to die from, I thought.

"So Ana has news," Mom said, cuing me to tell Dad about me mushing.

He didn't say anything at first, and then he began to nod. "Great! My daughter the musher." He squeezed my shoulders. "Good for you."

The timer went off. Once the cookies were out and cooling on the baking rack, Mom and Dad both reached for one.

"Wait! You're sure you want to eat them?" I asked. I pleaded with my eyes for them not to take one.

"They're fine, really," Mom said. "Are you going to eat one, Ana?"

"I guess," I said, sighing and taking one. If they were going to die, I might as well, too.

After they each took a bite of their cookie, I nibbled a crumb off mine. *They're your own germs*, I told myself.

I wondered how long it took for bacteria to make someone sick.

And I had to keep wondering—all night. I waited through dinner, praying that neither of my parents would keel over into their plates of Tuna, Crab, and Feta Casserole. And I actually poked Dad with a pencil during the ten o'clock news to make sure he was just sleeping and not a victim of poisoned cookie-dough batter. But none of us had so much as a hair fall out. Nothing.

Chapter 20

On Saturday morning, it was actually snowing, even though it was only November. Just great. Dad dropped me off at the Hopkinses' to begin my sled dog training.

Dasher met me by the dog yard. She had a plastic bag wrapped over her ankle bandage. "Isn't this snow great?" She put up her hands in amazement. "Four inches! We get to use the sled instead of the rig! Well, *you* get to use it. Ready?"

"Yeah, ready?" Cubby asked, coming out of the dog pen holding Noodles.

Dasher rolled her eyes. "Now, because of my stupid ankle, Cubby's going to have to show you what to do."

I was going to be trained by a just-barely-five-year-old?

"First: how to stand," Dasher said.

Cubby went over to the sled and hopped onto the two runners.

"Your turn, Ana," Dasher started.

"Hey—I'm in charge," Cubby whined.

"No, *I'm* in charge—I just need *you* to demo everything."

Cubby stomped his foot, and his lower lip wobbled like he was about to cry.

"Fine, fine," Dasher said. "Go ahead, Cubby."

He smiled. "Okay . . . Your turn, Ana."

I looked at the sled.

"Step on," Dasher and Cubby both said.

I walked over to the sled and stepped onto the runners.

"They're so far apart," I said, looking down at my feet.

"I guess. Anyway, hold onto the handlebar."

I grazed the wooden bar with my fingertips—my usual, OCD, less-is-more pose.

"No, *really* hold on," Cubby said, putting his hands on mine to get me to squeeze.

"Oh, let me just put my gloves on," I said, wondering when the handlebar was last scrubbed down.

As I was pulling on the second glove, Cubby continued, "Now, keep one foot on the runner and put the other on the brake—"

"Wait, where's the brake?"

"—then pull up the snow hook."

"Snow hook? What? Where?"

"Then—"

"Wait, you're going too fast!" I said, panicking. "I can't do this!" I stepped off the runners.

"Yes, you can," Dasher said, hopping closer to me. "Cubby, slow down. Ana, you can do this. Seriously. Okay, see that thing?" She pointed to a hook stuck in the snow like an anchor. "That's the—"

"Snow hook," Cubby said. "That's the snow hook. *I'm* helping her."

"Well, then, *slow down*," Dasher told him.

Dasher and Cubby had me practice raising and lowering the sled brake and setting the snow hook, making me bend back to pull it out of the ground over and over.

My gloves ended up super muddy from the mix of snow and dirt, but I figured I could throw them out when I got home.

"Of course, you always want to set the snow hook in front of your feet, or it could hook your leg if it comes loose," Dasher said. "You also want to get off the sled on the side opposite of the snow hook because, if it did come loose, it could hook you, and you could get dragged with the dogs." She must have seen the panic in my face because she added, "But I'm sure that won't happen. Just remember how to set it."

I gulped. This was complicated. And it wasn't like a recipe where, if I made a mistake, the result just tasted bad. If I messed this up, I could end up falling off the sled and losing a limb.

So on and on we went. Dasher had me practice the brake as well as steering right, then left, then right, over and over and over.

After lunch, Dasher decided I was ready to try it with dogs.

We walked into the dog pen and Dasher looked around. "I'm still not positive who'd be the best leaders for you . . ."

Some of the dogs jumped on top of their doghouses and started barking like they hoped to be chosen.

"Let's start with . . . Tulip. She can be your command leader. She's a good listener and stays on task pretty well."

And she's incredibly slow, I remembered Mr. Hopkins saying. For my sake, that was a good thing.

Dasher hooked her up to a leash and Cubby walked her to the drop chain so she could wait for us.

"Let's get a male for your other lead. Follow me," Dasher said, hopping over to the boy pen on her good foot. She tapped her glove on her lip and then smiled, her eyes lighting up. "Dracula—he'll be a perfect match with Tulip."

I wasn't sure which dog was Dracula, but I didn't think I wanted to use a dog named after a vampire while traveling alone through the woods.

I made A's into my hand. "Or what about Tulip and *Sweet Pea* as leaders?" I suggested. Their names even sounded pretty together.

"No way. Anyways, Tulip doesn't lead well with other females—she goes wild. Cubby, go get Dracula."

Don't, Cubby! I could picture the dog diving for my neck the minute he saw me to suck my blood.

But as Cubby brought him over, I laughed. *"That's* Dracula?" He was scrawny and mellow, and didn't look like a typical sled dog at all. His back half was black, and his front half was mostly white with almost a triangle shape of black between his eyes— kind of like the real Dracula's widow's peak.

"He's a Eurohound," Dasher explained. "One of my dad's sprint dogs, but he's slower now that he's old. He'll be fine for you though."

We went over to where Tulip was waiting on the drop line.

"Why don't you harness Tulip first?" Dasher said.

"Come here, Tulip," I said, taking hold of her collar. I gently slipped the harness over her head while she tried to wiggle out of it. "It's okay, Tulip. Come on."

"Correct her," Dasher said.

"No, Tulip," I said, petting her.

"No!" Dasher snapped.

I stopped.

"That was for Tulip. You have to say it like you're in charge," she said.

"No!" I shouted.

"But don't yell at her."

"Right." Luckily, Tulip cooperated after that.

After we got Dracula harnessed too, I practiced steering again with the snow hook solidly planted so the dogs couldn't go anywhere.

Tulip and Dracula were very patient, standing there. Tulip only tried to run twice.

"Tomorrow we'll work on going forward," Dasher said.

"What about using Sweet Pea instead of *Tulip*?" I suggested.

"Oh no, no, no," Dasher said. "Sweet Pea's never pulled before. She'd have no idea what she was doing."

Especially if she never gets the chance, I thought.

Chapter 21

Dasher told me to take a hot bath when I got home to relax my muscles, and it didn't take me long to figure out why. That afternoon, I could hardly move, I was so sore from bending over to lift and plant the snow hook.

Luckily, I could still bake. Lily came over and we had a bake-a-rama, whipping up all different kinds of cookies to make up for all the time we missed out on.

While we were working on some peppermint cut-out cookies shaped like dog bones, I said, "Maybe I could give some of these out at the race."

Lily drizzled peppermint glaze over one of the cookies. "Yeah, and we can try making edible dog bowls to have them displayed in. Right?"

I smiled. "Maybe out of . . . marshmallow and rice cereal?"

She nodded and started getting out the ingredients. It was like we shared a baking brain.

"How's dog training going?" she asked.

I laughed. "I'm not sure whether I could say *I'm* training the dogs—more like *they're* training me. It's a lot harder than I thought it would be."

"I wish I could help, but I have that catering job."

"I know. I'm not sure what you could do for me besides mushing in my place anyway."

"No, thanks. I just painted my nails." She held up her tannish-yellow fingernails. "What do you think of the color? First I used a milk-chocolate–colored polish, and then a yellow. I call the color 'buttered toast.'"

"Nice." I never painted my fingernails—polish only hid the dirt that could be beneath them.

"Anyway, if you ever want to help Via and me out at one of our catering gigs, it'd be awesome."

"I wish. I'm training with Dasher nonstop until the race."

"She could come, too. She seems pretty cool."

"Yeah, I guess," I mumbled. But I still wanted it to just be Lily and me.

By nighttime, my back felt like I had used a lemon juicer on it. Mom warmed up a rice-filled heating pad for me.

"You're really taking this race seriously," she said as she removed the bag from the microwave.

"Well, I don't have a choice—it's for school. Mr. Creed would flunk me for sure if I didn't do this."

"I doubt that." She handed me the warm bag, and I wiggled my back around until it was in the right spot. "How's your ERP going?" she asked. "Are you still reading your script?"

"I don't need to read that one anymore." At least not for now. My OCD was like ocean waves. The worries came and went, but sometimes they came back like a tsunami.

"Is there anything else that's bothering you? I can help you write a new script if you want."

I hadn't thought about the whole bloody corn syrup incident in a while—I was finally over it. I'd absolutely never get over Bernie dying, but I was getting closer to accepting it. And being friends with Lily again, well, that helped everything. "Nope," I said. "I don't need any right now."

"What about working with the dogs? Are you having any anxiety about them? I remember the first time you came home from Dasher's and one had licked you—"

I burst out laughing. "I totally forgot about Luna kissing me! But, no, I'm fine about the dogs."

She shrugged. "The mystery of OCD, I suppose."

The next morning, I went back to Dasher's to practice again.

When I got there, Cubby already had Tulip harnessed.

"Today you'll be traveling," Dasher said. "Just straight, of course."

"What if Tulip and Dracula take off running, and I fall off?" I wrapped my arms around myself.

"The most important thing is to not let the dogs and the sled get away. Try to get back on, step down on the brake, and say 'Whoa!'" Dasher said, checking Tulip's harness. "But Tulip wouldn't do that to you. Right, Tulip?"

She blinked, and her ears flattened against her head.

I wished I understood dog.

Cubby and I hooked Tulip and Dracula up to the sled.

Cubby demonstrated how to get them going. Then it was my turn.

I took a step back and wrapped my arms around myself. "Are you sure they know what they're doing?" I looked at Tulip—she licked her lips and wagged her tail.

Dasher laughed. "Tulip's been mushing since she was a pup. She's seven now. And Dracula's an old pro."

I wasn't sure if seven years was a long time or not, but it was a lot longer than I had been mushing.

"And my dad's going to watch because you're new and he doesn't want you to fall off and get dragged or something. Not that you would." She smiled. "Seriously, this is totally safe. He's just there to . . . give you pointers afterward."

I looked over at Mr. Hopkins, who was getting his four-wheeler out of the barn.

I waved to him to make sure he saw me, in case I became a human ragdoll with sled dogs attached to me. "Here I go." I stepped on the runners.

"Lift the snow hook and let up on the brake," Dasher told me. "Make sure you're balanced, though. Then say 'Hike!' and be sure you're holding on to the handlebar. When you get to the end of the barn, say 'Whoa!' and have them stop. And don't forget—never let go!"

"Right. Never let go," I said.

As I tried to remember whether to pick up the snow hook or brake first, I noticed Dasher snapping pictures with her phone.

"We need photos for our backboard," she explained.

"Let me look like I halfway know what I'm doing first," I said.

Dracula looked back at me like, "Let's go already."

I timidly lifted the snow hook and lightened up on the brake.

Quick breaths.

"What are you waiting for?" Cubby asked. "Go!"

"Okay. Um . . . go!" I said. "I mean, hike!" I grabbed on to the handlebar as Tulip and Dracula pulled the sled forward and it jerked to a start. "Slow down! Slow down!"

"Slow down?" I heard Cubby say to Dasher. "They're hardly moving!"

"I know, but she's new," Dasher said. "Ana, you're doing fine."

"Okay," I said. "Keep going, Tulip. Just don't do anything crazy."

We finally began to slide through the snow—not really fast, but we were actually moving. I froze in the position I was in. So far, so good.

"You're doing great!" Dasher shouted to me.

As we got closer to the barn, the dogs began to speed up.

"Wait! Slow down! Um . . . gee!" I shouted, forgetting what command meant what. "Gee! Now!"

The dogs kept going fast and turned to the right.

"No—not gee. Slow down! Help, Dasher! I can't remember the commands!" I shouted out. "Haw, Tulip! I mean whoa!" I began pushing down on the brake. They veered in the other direction and then stopped.

"Phew," I said, trying to catch my breath and wipe my sweaty forehead.

"Don't get off without setting the hook!" Mr. Hopkins called out.

I shoved the snow hook into the snowy ground. *Get off the sled on the side opposite the snow hook . . .*

Finally, back on land.

I scratched the top of Tulip's head. "We did it!" I rubbed Dracula's ears. "We're still alive!" He gave me a blank stare.

"Oh, jeez, Ana," Dasher started as she made her way to us. "Are you okay?"

I nodded. "I think so."

"Maybe we should go through commands again?" she suggested, grabbing Tulip's collar.

"Yeah, that's a good idea."

Mushing was no piece of cake—and definitely not as easy as making one.

After a very long day, which included two panic-inducing episodes where Cubby had to hop on the sled to help me, I sat at my computer, searching for some other project Dasher and I could do instead. There was no way I could mush. I liked the idea of sled dog racing and all, but to be in charge of a team of dogs through the woods, on two thin boards, by myself? We *had* to change our project. Maybe we could do it on the same topic Mr. Creed's son did—he'd probably like that. I could ask for a microscope as an early Christmas gift.

I sighed and emailed Grammy about my fear of mushing.

> Dear Ana,
>   Oh dear! That sounds scary.
>   Have you ever looked at a recipe and thought it would be impossible to make? What helped you get through it?
> Love,
> Grammy

I thought for a minute. After my Great-Aunt Katja had passed away, I was given her recipe collection. She was from Slovenia and had a box full of recipes that had been passed down from generations before she came to America. Some were really complicated—one in particular.

Potica Nut Roll, I wrote back.

What helped me get through it? I thought a minute. Looking at one step at a time.

Dear Ana,
    Do the same for the dogs-on-sleds racing.
Love,
Grammy

I sighed deeply and closed my laptop, and then I went to the kitchen and got out the carton of eggs.

"What are you making?" Dad asked. "And when will it be done? Because I'm ready to eat it."

"Potica," I said, getting out the raisins and walnuts. "And it won't be ready for a while. Some things take a lot of time and practice to get right."

"And that's just fine," he said and patted my arm. "I'm sure it will be worth it."

Chapter 22

After a couple more days of traveling straight, Dasher and Cubby showed me how to turn corners. Then, once Tulip, Dracula, and I got pretty good at it, Dasher mixed things up.

"Time to add a third dog," she said.

"What? Why?" I petted Tulip's fur. The three of us had become quite a team.

"Because you don't want to be in the baby category, that's why."

"Hey, I race with two dogs. I'm not a baby!" Cubby cried.

"Whatever, Cubby." Dasher turned toward me. "Biscuit can be your wheel dog."

Biscuit was mostly white but had biscuit-colored splotches

on her back and honey-colored ears. She stood tall and wore a bored expression.

"All right, then . . ." I said.

We hooked up all three dogs.

"Now, there are more things to remember with three dogs than two," she said. "First, when connecting them to the lines, you want to be sure the harnesses . . ."

Great-Aunt Katja's potica, I told myself, remembering Grammy's advice. *One step at a time.*

At lunch on Monday, Lily and Via told me all about their first catering job for Lily's mom's book club. Since it was a brunch, Lily had made a cheese frittata, and Via had planned to make banana bread from a box.

"I didn't want to wait the sixty minutes for it to cook," Via said, eating a packaged sandwich again, "so I put the oven temp on four-fifty instead of three-fifty. That way, I figured I'd only have to wait forty-six minutes."

"She's really good at math," Lily added.

"Well, the top was brown in twenty minutes, so I took it out of the oven. I decided to wait to slice it until I got to Lily's so it would still be warm for the meeting." Via paused to remove the pickles from her sandwich and set them in a pile on the cafeteria table. "I go to cut it, and it's completely liquid on the inside. It was like soup."

Hmm . . . banana soup . . .

"Luckily," Via continued, "we had Lily's frittata. I ended up making toast as the guests were coming in the door."

Toast? Wow, Lily must have died. We never made plain toast.

"But we were still asked to do another event," Lily said. "My mom's friend, Mrs. Rodriguez, said she was impressed with the whole idea and with my frittata, and she wants us to cater her next crocheting meeting. I'm thinking we should do some kind of theme . . . like Winter-White Wonderland or Festa Italiana or something."

I smiled, although I could feel my cheeks burning. I could think up five wintery recipes in my head on the spot.

"Any ideas for us, Ana?" Via asked, eating the pickle slices off the table.

I shook my head, trying to ignore all the pickled germs she was eating. As much as I wanted to help Lily, I still wasn't ready to have Via using my ideas.

"Let's meet this weekend to start a list," Via said to Lily.

Here we go again. Me, the third wheel.

I looked over at Dasher sitting on the other side of the cafeteria, reading some mushing book while eating a cafeteria hotdog.

I could go sit with her for the rest of lunch . . .

But then she set her book down, opened a ketchup packet, and began squirting it all over her hotdog.

Now I couldn't go over there! I lowered my eyes.

"So, can you help us?" Lily asked, elbowing me.

"Huh? Oh. I can't. I need to try running the dogs in booties. And I need to work up to mushing at least half a mile."

"The dogs wear booties?" Via laughed. "That's hysterical!"

"Well, just for practice . . ."

"Maybe you can come over afterward," Lily added. "We're going to cheerleading tryouts right after school, anyway."

"Cheerleading?" I asked.

Lily nodded. "You want to try out, too?

Having a whole crowd watch me as I tried to remember a cheer? "That's okay."

"Do you wanna come over tonight, though?"

It would be fun to help Lily think up recipes, but I did have to get ready for my race. My grade depended on it. And, anyway, Via would be there. "No, seriously, I need to train. Considering how long it took me to harness the team myself, I can't imagine what it'll take to put booties on twelve moving paws."

The bell rang. "See ya," Via said.

"So you're going to try out for cheerleading?" I asked Lily, closing my lunch bag.

She shrugged. "Why not?"

"But we don't like cheerleading."

"*You* might not, but maybe *I* do," she said. "People change, you know?"

I nodded as if I understood. But I didn't. I hadn't changed. Why did she have to?

Chapter 23

Thursday was Thanksgiving. I spent the day helping Mom with the meal, adding my own special touches to her traditional dishes. Dad said my Mushed Potatoes were his favorite.

Friday, I baked another batch of finger-touched cookie dough. It wasn't as horrible as the first time but still pretty scary.

Then I went to Dasher's to practice. After all that, I was ready to have a good run in the snow. Wow, I even *thought* like a musher now.

When I got there, Dasher met me at the door.

"You're going to have to train with just Cubby today," she said. "My mom's making me finish my homework before I can go outside this weekend. Did you do your English essay yet?"

I nodded. "A week ago."

"Well, I'll come out when I finish."

Cubby came to the door with Noodles in his hand. "I'm ready to train you." He bounced on his toes with excitement. "Mom, we're going outside," he yelled into the kitchen.

"Call me when you're ready to hit the trail," she called back.

We walked out to the yard.

"So, you have to listen to me because I'm in charge," Cubby said.

I turned my head away to snicker as we approached the dog pen.

"Hi, Sweet Pea," I said, scratching her behind her ears. "I wish you could be part of my team." She wagged her tail at me. Then I realized a perk to training with Cubby. "Hey, want to see if Sweet Pea can race?"

"But your team is Tulip, Dracula, and Biscuit," Cubby said.

"Yeah, but don't you think Sweet Pea would make a good leader? I think she would. I'd just take out Dracula."

"But Dasher said that Tulip—"

"But *you're* in charge, right?" I said. "Dasher said so."

A smile spread across Cubby's face. "Yeah, I'm in charge. Not Dasher."

"And wouldn't she be surprised if Sweet Pea and Tulip turned out to be an awesome pair?"

He thought for a moment and then grinned. "Let's try her," he said.

I anchored the sled to a pole while Cubby got Biscuit and

hooked her up. "I'll get Tulip, and you can get Sweet Pea," he said.

But as I brought Sweet Pea closer to Tulip and Biscuit, she yanked her leash in the opposite direction, forcing me to stop and park my feet in the snow so she didn't pull me over. Why was she being so stubborn?

"It's okay," I said, trying again to get her over to the dogs, but she just pulled back harder. "I know you're nervous, but—"

Tulip and Biscuit barked at her. "Jeez, you guys know Sweet Pea. Why are you barking at her?" I began sliding Sweet Pea's harness on.

"Stop squirming, Sweet Pea," Cubby whined. He helped me hook her onto the neck line next to Tulip, who bared her teeth at her. I realized then that maybe it wasn't such a good idea, but we were in too deep. As I was about to clip Sweet Pea onto the tug line, Tulip growled and snapped at her.

"No!" I shouted, not sure what to do.

"Stop! Stop!" Cubby yelled. Biscuit began barking, too, and Sweet Pea squirmed right out of her harness. Before I could stop her, she took off.

"No, Sweet Pea! Come back!" I cried, chasing after her. "Stop! Please, stop!" But she just kept running and running, her leash trailing behind her.

Dasher hobbled out of the house. "Why are you guys yelling? What happened?"

"Sweet Pea! She got loose!" I said and pointed in the direction she ran. Cubby began sprinting after her, but that only seemed to make her run faster. "Cubby—stop! You're scaring her!" But it was too late. Sweet Pea ran into the woods and out of sight.

"Wait—Sweet Pea? What was she even doing out of the pen?" Dasher said.

"Everything all right out here?" Mrs. Hopkins asked, running out the back door. "What's going on?"

"Sweet Pea. She ran off," I said, my voice quivering.

"Oh, no," she said. "Ana and Cubby, get the other dogs back into their pens. Then get some treats and squeaky toys—maybe she'll come if she hears a familiar sound. Cubby, I'll talk to you later about why Sweet Pea was hooked up in the first place. Dasher, wait here in case she comes back." Mrs. Hopkins looked at her watch. "I hope we find her soon—we have to leave for Cubby's piano recital in an hour."

"I'm so sorry, Mrs. Hopkins," I said.

"I know, honey. Let's start looking." She went to the barn, hopped onto their four-wheeler, and headed into the woods.

Cubby and I brought Biscuit and Tulip back to the pen and then ran to the house. "I'm still in charge, you know," he told me. "I think there's a squeaker toy under my bed. I'll go look. You get her treats."

"Where are they?" I asked, opening their kitchen cabinets.

"I use them as breadcrumbs when I play Hansel and Gretel. Look under the couch."

"You mean in this pouch?" I shouted to him in the other room. I went to open the paper pouch he had made, and it sliced across my finger.

"Ouch!" I cried.

"You find it?" he shouted back.

I looked down at my finger. A thin line of blood was starting to form on the paper cut. Spreading my own germs was almost as bad as getting other people's germs on me. I was about to drip my insides onto their carpet.

"Cool, you're bleeding!" Cubby said, looking over my shoulder.

"I've got to clean up," I said and hurried to the bathroom sink, cradling my finger with my other hand.

"Hurry up, Ana," Cubby said, holding Noodles.

"I am. I am," I said as I ran my finger under the water. I didn't want to get my blood on Sweet Pea when we found her.

Come on, Ana. You need to get outside and look for Sweet Pea.

Rinse, soap, rinse. Rinse, soap, rinse.

"You sure use a lot of soap," Cubby said. "My mom doesn't let me use that much."

"I don't want to get an infection." *Rinse, soap, rinse. Rinse, soap, rinse.* Then I remembered that I wasn't in my own bathroom. I was leaving microscopic blood cells all over the place—I could get the whole Hopkins family sick.

Hurry! You've got to find Sweet Pea.

I opened the medicine cabinet, found some bandages, and quickly put them on.

Then I squirted some liquid soap onto a tissue and, in record speed, cleaned the sink, faucet handles, and the pump on the liquid soap.

"You're cleaning the soap?" Cubby asked, making Noodles wave at me.

"Sorry, I just . . . have to." Oh, this was awful. "Do you think Sweet Pea got very far?"

"Nah. Tulip gets loose all the time. She's always just saying hi to the boy dogs."

Yeah, but this was Sweet Pea. I didn't see her being real social with the other dogs.

I wanted to sanitize everything one more time, even though I could picture Sweet Pea running farther and farther away. *Come on Ana! Remember your ERP therapy and GET PAST THE CONTAMINATED-BATHROOM ISSUE.*

My OCD brain wanted me to clean the sink at least one more time, but I had to ignore it. Sweet Pea was more important. I'd have to assume the Hopkinses' bathroom was fine, even though it was killing me inside. I could do round two after we found her.

I threw the paper towel out and said, "Come on."

As Cubby got on his bike, I hurried over to Dasher, who was hopping her way out of the barn.

"She's not in there," she said. "Why was Sweet Pea out while you were setting up the sled, anyway?"

I cringed.

Dasher looked at Cubby and then at me. "No, you didn't! *You tried to hook up Sweet Pea?*"

"Well, yeah, but—" I started, although I didn't have a good explanation.

"What were you thinking? I told you she can't run with a team. You've seen how skittish she is!"

"I know. I'm sorry." I blinked back tears. "I guess I wasn't thinking—I have a lot going on right now. With learning to mush, and getting you ready for the pancake breakfast, and—"

"*You* have a lot going on? How do you think I feel? I move all the way to Illinois—away from my home and friends, where my dogs only get to practice a couple months of the year. And then I don't even get to race!"

She took a step closer to me. I'd never seen her angry before—her eyes were narrowed and her neck was as red as cherry syrup. I stepped back.

"Not only that," she continued, "but my so-called *friend*—a friend who pretends to be helping someone with a math test so she doesn't have to sit with me at lunch, even though I've never seen her doing work then—loses one of my dogs! Yeah, some friend."

My jaw dropped. I wanted to respond—but I had nothing to say.

"And I won't even go into how anyone who knows *anything* about mushing would *never* put a dog like Sweet Pea *as a lead* the first time out, as well as next to Tulip, who I told you doesn't like to run next to another female. That is, if you were even listening to me." She put her hand up. "I think you should go." As her eyes filled with tears, she turned away.

"Dasher, please. I want to help look—"

"Get out of here!"

My own tears began to flow as I walked back into their house to get my things. How did I let this happen? Dasher had warned me about Sweet Pea. And now she'd never forgive me.

"Sweet Pea!" I called out. No answer. I started to go in the back door to call home and stopped. I bit my lip.

I can't leave with Sweet Pea lost.

So while Dasher wasn't looking, I took off to find her.

Chapter 24

I saw Mrs. Hopkins return to the barn empty-handed as I was slipping into the woods where Sweet Pea had escaped. I put my hands on my hips and exhaled. No way was I coming back without her.

The woods looked different than when we'd mushed through them. The bare trees appeared wicked and gnarled—like they could swallow me up.

Where would a dog go if she was afraid of her own shadow?

Well, not along the open trail. I took a deep breath and stepped off it.

It was almost dinnertime, and pretty dark already. Under

a canopy of trees, it might as well have been the middle of the night.

What I wouldn't give for Sweet Pea to still be curled up in her doghouse at Dasher's so I could be home, snuggled up on the couch.

"Sweet Pea!" I called out.

I listened for a whimper or the jingle of her collar.

Besides the frigid whisper of the wind, it was silent. Eerily so.

Keeping my head low, I looked for clues. There always seemed to be some in detective shows: fur, a broken collar, footprints in the snow, something. But I found nothing.

"Sweet Pea!" I called out. "Sweet Pea—I have a treat for you!"

Dasher had been right about her. About everything. And why hadn't I invited Dasher to our lunch table? Maybe we really were friends. Why didn't I think of her that way?

I sighed.

And then there was innocent, timid Sweet Pea who was missing because of me and my stupid idea to have her run.

Don't worry, I said to myself. *Sweet Pea will turn up.*

It was getting so dark it was hard to make my way around. I wished I'd gone into the Hopkinses' house and grabbed my phone to text Lily before I went into the woods. She could've met me out here. And brought a flashlight.

No, this was my mess. I needed to clean it up myself.

Whooo! Whoooo!

An owl! Did they eat people? Or dogs? And what about bats? Were they out here, too?

I looked up at the dark sky, and a single star twinkled back at me. *Bernie*, I thought. I wasn't alone after all.

I could do this. I stepped around a huge branch on the ground, my boots crunching in the snow. The woods were kind of a mess with branches and sticks. But maybe a dog would like it like this—lots of places to hide.

Finally, I heard a rustling from behind me. "Sweet Pea?"

The sound was getting closer, but all I could make out was a shadowed figure—way too tall and loud for little Sweet Pea. It was a person! Or a bear!

"Who's there?" I said, trying to sound as confident as I could, even though my heart was racing four hundred beats per second. "I have my watch dog with me. *Woof, woof*," I barked as best I could.

A flashlight glared in my eyes. "Ana?"

It was Dasher. Her shadow had made her look taller than she was. I breathed a sigh of relief. "Jeez—you scared me!"

"You found Sweet Pea? Where is she?" she asked, shining her flashlight around me.

"No, not yet."

"What are you doing out here? I thought you went home."

"Yeah, well." I paused. "I'm so sorry about what happened."

"You should be." Dasher started walking again, using a stick as a cane for her ankle. I hesitated, then followed her. "That was a super bad idea."

"I know. But I'm going to find her, I promise. I'm so worried about her, Dasher! It's freezing out."

Dasher sighed. "She's got thick fur—she always sleeps outside, remember? But if she's out here too long, she could get hungry or hurt."

I began drawing A's in my hand.

"But," Dasher continued, "she's such a scaredy cat, she probably didn't get very far. We'll find her." She pulled her backpack higher onto her back. "Let's look over by that patch of pine trees."

Dasher waved her flashlight around, and I called out. We walked around and around for what felt like hours.

"Wait!" I said, "I hear something."

There was a rustle of leaves to our left, then a raccoon or some other chubby forest-dweller scurried off.

"Let's try over here," Dasher said, and we turned right.

"So, I thought you were going to Cubby's recital," I said, peering behind a log.

"I was. But I told my parents my ankle hurt too bad, and I stayed home."

I looked down at it. "Where's your brace?"

"I didn't want it to slow me down." She stopped walking. "Wait, what about you? Do your parents know what you're doing?"

"Not exactly." I pulled my gloves out of my coat pockets and slipped them on. "I'm hoping they'll think our practice ran long."

"Long? It's, like, seven o'clock."

"It's just . . . I have to find Sweet Pea."

"I know," she said. "You guys are so tight. That's why I'm out here."

"Because of me?"

She nodded and then cleared her throat. "Try calling to her again."

"Sweet Pea! Sweet Pea!" I called out, and we waited. Nothing. "Sweet Pea!"

I pictured a bird's-eye view of the woods, then zoomed out to imagine the entire earth. She could be anywhere on the planet.

Sweet Pea was probably cowering somewhere, too terrified to come out to eat. She was already shy, and that was with the Hopkinses, who were the best dog parents ever.

I missed her. And I thought she must miss me, too. We needed each other. We were the same—two scaredy-cats.

After an eternity, Dasher whispered, "Over there!" She pointed her flashlight at the bottom of a tree. Something gold glittered back at us—a dog collar. Sweet Pea!

There she was, scrunched up in the hollow of a tree, her tail curled around her body.

The problem was, there was a deathly obstacle course blocking her—a maze of branches and a huge, fallen tree. And we couldn't walk around the tree with a ravine to the side of it.

"You hold the flashlight," Dasher whispered, passing it to me. "And I'll go get her."

I looked over at Sweet Pea again. I knew if we called her to come, she might run. But if Dasher tried to get her, she might also run. And Dasher had her bad ankle . . .

I bit my lip.

I couldn't save Bernie, but I could save Sweet Pea.

"I'll get her."

I handed the flashlight back to Dasher.

"Okay, go real slow so you don't scare her," Dasher told me.

I nodded.

"Here." She handed me a small bag of ultra-smelly dog food. "Liver treats. Dogs can't resist them."

I put the liver in my pocket.

Where to even begin. Low-hanging branches were everywhere. Every time I pushed one away from my face, there'd be another one ready to poke my eye out or give me tetanus.

I squeezed between prickly branches, hoping I wouldn't rip my jacket.

"Good, good," Dasher said quietly. "Now, you're right by that big fallen tree. You'll have to crawl over it."

The flashlight cast just a thin beam of light. I felt my way over to the tree. It was really big! I sat on it and tried to swing my legs around. My boot was caught on something. As I yanked my foot loose, the boot came off and went flying through the air.

"I'll get it," Dasher said. "You get Sweet Pea."

I grimaced as I put my left foot down and it skidded in a muddy, slushy mess. My sock was covered in yuckiness, and now my foot was wet. Could I die from mud exposure? I'd surely get a bacterial infection, at least. Or hypothermia.

That's your OCD talking, I told myself. *Just keep going.*

"Almost there," Dasher said. "Sweet Pea's watching you."

I stepped over a prickly bush, finally reaching the tree.

I crouched down next to Sweet Pea, pulling the bag of food out of my pocket. "Are you hungry?"

Her tail thumped fast.

I dumped some food into my gloved hand. She poked her head out from inside the tree, sniffed my hand, and then scarfed up the food.

"Omigod. Sweet Pea! I'm so happy we found you!" I squealed, putting my arms around her furry body. "Did you miss me?" She thumped her tail again.

I ran my fingers down her back. "Are you all right?" I looked her over. Her paws were all muddy—like my foot—but otherwise she seemed okay.

I held onto her collar and navigated the mess of branches back over to Dasher. She set down my boot and clipped a leash onto Sweet Pea's collar. "There. Gotcha, you little runaway. You're in big trouble." She scratched Sweet Pea behind her ears. "Your foot went right in that mud puddle, huh? You should probably take your sock off, or you could get frostbite."

I pulled it off. Now what?

"Just stick your boot back on. You can borrow a pair of socks at my house."

I put my boot on my bare foot, realizing I'd have to try to clean the dirt out when I got home. I held up the dripping, wet sock.

"Throw it in your pocket," she said.

"Of my coat?"

She took it from my hand and shoved it into her own pocket. "Let's go," she said, pulling on Sweet Pea's leash a little.

"I'll take her," I said. Dasher handed me the leash, and I finally relaxed a little. "Thanks."

"For what? *You* got her."

"We both did," I said.

"Let's hurry back before my folks get home."

As we began to leave the woods, Dasher started to walk in the opposite direction as me.

"Wait," I said. "Don't you live that way?"

"Nuh-uh. I live this way."

"But we just came from over there." I pointed to where we had found Sweet Pea.

"Oh yeah," she said, turning around.

But that didn't help much. When we were looking for Sweet Pea, we had made all sorts of turns—pretty much whenever we heard a noise.

"Hmm." Dasher waved her flashlight in a circle.

"Can't you use your phone's GPS?" I asked.

"Nah. My phone is only a phone. What about yours?"

"I left it at your house. Let's call your parents and have them find us."

She shook her head. "First, they're probably not home yet. Second, I'm not supposed to be out here with my bad ankle. And third, what if they panic and send the police or a forest ranger looking for us? We'll just figure out the way."

"But aren't these woods part of the forest preserve?" I asked. "And the forest preserve is, like, miles and miles. If we start heading in the wrong direction, we could end up in the middle of nowhere."

"No, I think I have some idea which way to go now," she said. "But you better call home anyway before your mom comes to pick you up or something. You can say you're spending the night at my house."

Lying and walking blindly through the forest at night definitely weren't things I wanted to do, but this time, I'd have to trust Dasher. After what happened with Sweet Pea, I owed her that much.

I took her phone. "Hi, Mom," I said when she picked up. "Yeah, sorry I didn't call sooner. We've been practicing. Um, I wondered if I could spend the night here?"

"Really? Do you *want* to spend the night?"

"Yeah."

"Does she know about some of your . . . bedtime procedures?" Mom asked.

I turned away from Dasher, hoping she couldn't hear the conversation. "I'll figure it out. Can I?"

"I suppose. I'll pick you up around ten tomorrow morning. Or do you think you two will want to sleep in?"

"No, I'll call you," I said. "I better go."

"I'm so proud of you," Mom said.

"Why?"

"For trying new things and making new friends."

If she only knew what a horrible friend I'd been.

"All right," Dasher said after I hung up. "Let's try this way first."

Chapter 25

Dasher and I walked for about a half an hour, until all she could do was limp.

"Did you bring any water?" Dasher asked, stopping.

I shook my head.

"We can all share mine, then." She opened her backpack and got out a bottle. "Here, you go first."

I was about to take a sip when I remembered there wasn't a bathroom in the woods. I shook my head. "Sweet Pea can have my portion."

"All right." Dasher held the bottle up to Sweet Pea's mouth and let her lap up water from it. Once Sweet Pea was done, Dasher drank some, and we started walking again. The wind had picked up, snow was coming down, and my fingers were super cold. I put up my coat's hood.

Nothing really looked familiar, but I hadn't paid much attention when I was trying to find Sweet Pea.

Dasher sighed. "Can we stop again? My ankle's killing me." She looked around. "Let's sit here."

We secured Sweet Pea's leash to a tree. She walked in a circle before plopping down into a little ball.

Dasher pulled a sweatshirt out of her backpack and laid it down on the ground. "Here, you can sit on this if you want."

I paused for a minute. Anything could be on the ground: microscopic parasites, ticks looking for host bodies . . .

But I was tired.

Here goes nothing. I sat down before I could change my mind.

"I'm starving," Dasher said. "You have anything to eat?"

"No. Do you?"

She reached into her coat pocket and pulled a bunch of stuff out. "Let's see . . . ABC gum in an old quiz, dog treats, and . . . yay! I still have some of your Musher Mix."

Dasher handed me the bag of trail mix. But sharing food was just one step too far after everything else I'd braved that day. I passed it back.

The bandages on my hand were getting all wet and yucky, so I yanked them off and shoved them in my coat pocket.

"What a day, huh?" she said, tipping her head and pouring trail mix into her mouth right out of the bag.

I slid off my boot to examine my dirty foot. At least it was dry now. "I'm just glad we found Sweet Pea." I checked my glands. Not swollen yet.

"Me too. Sorry I blew up at you this afternoon. It wasn't just about Sweet Pea. I was upset that you were getting to race instead of me. And then my mom wouldn't even let me outside to help you train because of my never-ending homework."

She sighed and continued. "Sled dog racing is everything to me. I mean, back home, dogs were my life. I totally miss being in Alaska." She took another sip of water. "I wish it didn't bother me that much, but it does."

"Really?" I was surprised that anything bothered her.

"It's just not the same here. I guess that's why I kind of I forced you to do our project on sled dog racing. It's what keeps me sane." She laughed. "I hope you don't think I'm crazy or something."

Should I tell her about my OCD? What if she thought my cleaning and problems with red food and stuff were just too super weird? What if she told me to find my way home myself?

I looked at Sweet Pea, and she got up and came over to sit next to me. Sweet Pea trusted me. And so did Dasher. Even after I lost one of her dogs and left her sitting alone at lunch, she was willing to give me another chance.

"Um . . . I guess there's something you should know about me, too. I have OCD—obsessive-compulsive disorder. It makes me not like germs, and so I kind of wash my hands a lot."

Dasher didn't say anything.

"But," I continued, "it's not contagious or anything."

Dasher laughed a little. "Too bad. My mom's always getting on me about being cleaner."

"So . . . you're okay with it?" I drew A's into my hand on my lap.

She gave me a weird look. "What do you mean? Like, would I not be your friend because of it?"

I gulped. "Yeah, I guess."

"I knew you were kind of into cleaning stuff, but that's cool. You're a lot of fun, and you've been a good friend. Actually, you've been my only friend." Dasher played with the trail mix still in her hand. "It hasn't been easy moving here. In case you haven't noticed, people kind of think I'm strange because I dress different and don't do stuff like play soccer or cheerlead. You're the only person that gets me."

I ran my fingers through Sweet Pea's fur. It was funny how much Dasher and I were alike. "Sorry I never invited you to sit at my lunch table. I—"

She waved her hand in the air. "Yeah, forget I said anything. I'm *so* embarrassed I blurted that out—I say stupid stuff when I'm upset. I know you and Lily have been friends forever, so of course you want to sit with her at lunch."

"Yeah, but I should've invited you to sit with us," I said. "I guess I just hoped that me and Lily would always be best friends—and only us." Dasher looked down. "But," I continued, "I don't want to be friends with just Lily anymore—she's into cheerleading, and I'm not. And I'm into mushing, and she's not. We don't have to do everything together, you know?

"And anyway"—Sweet Pea started licking my hand—"Lily's friends with Via, now, too." *Lick, lick, lick.* "And I'm friends with you!" Sweet Pea licked my ear, and Dasher and I both started laughing.

"Sweet Pea really likes you," Dasher said, digging her hand into the bag of trail mix again and then offering me some. "If you hate germs so much, how come she doesn't bother you?"

I shrugged and grabbed a couple pieces of trail mix. "I don't know. She just doesn't. She makes me feel better, actually."

I told Dasher about Bernie Toast—how his germs never bothered me, and how he used to help me relax. "Now I have Sweet Pea for that."

"Well, it's cool you've bonded with her. She doesn't give anybody else the time of day."

"I'm super sorry about trying to mush with her. I thought she might enjoy racing. I just wanted her to have a chance. That's all," I explained.

"And now what do you think?" Dasher asked.

I ran my fingers through Sweet Pea's fur. "She's not a sled dog."

All of a sudden, there was a rustling in the woods. Sweet Pea heard it too and whined.

We sat perfectly still, listening. There was definitely something out there.

"Do you think it's a bear?" I asked.

"There aren't bears around here, goof. It's probably a coyote."

My heart went racing in my chest. "A coyote!" I popped up.

"Girls," a deep voice called through the trees.

"Dad?" Dasher shined the flashlight in the direction of the voice. It was Mr. Hopkins and my dad. They'd found us.

Oh—they'd *found us*, which meant they knew we had lied.

"Uh, hello," I said as if the whole situation weren't at all unusual.

"Dana Ruby Hopkins, what are you doing out here?" her dad said.

"First, are you two all right?" Dad asked.

We nodded. We were in such big trouble.

Mr. Hopkins continued. "That's good, at least. Now, Dasher, explain to me why you think the Morgans or I would allow you two out in the middle of the forest at night."

"We were going to be back home before you even knew we were gone," Dasher said, "but we got lost."

"And that makes it all right?" he asked.

"Sorry. It was all my idea," Dasher sniffled. "I . . . invited Ana to spend the night and then said we should go look for Sweet Pea."

I looked at her, surprised.

"Dasher," Mr. Hopkins said, "how irresponsible of you! And to not even tell us you invited Ana over. Ana's mother called, wanting to check in with her, and I didn't even know she was spending the night. Then, when I went into your bedroom, it was empty. You can only imagine the hysteria you two caused."

"It was my idea to keep looking after it got dark," I said. "Sorry." Now I had gotten Dasher in trouble, too. I bit my lip to keep from crying.

"Well, I don't even know where to start," Dad said. "But it's late. We'll deal with this in the morning."

The walk through woods back to the Hopkinses' was more silent and scary than when I was there alone. I hardly got to say goodbye to Dasher and Sweet Pea before Dasher's dad whisked her inside.

Once Dad and I got into the car, I pulled off my boots to warm my feet by the heater vent.

"So what do you have to say for yourself?" Dad asked as we pulled out of the Hopkinses' driveway.

I took a deep breath. "Sweet Pea escaped, and it was all my fault. I had no choice but to try to find her. Even if it meant going in the woods at night."

"I don't like that you lied to us."

I nodded. "I know. It won't happen again." I hung my head.

He snuck a quick peek at me and suppressed a grin. "You're quite a mess. You must really like that dog."

I looked down at my hands, which were caked in dirt. The knees of my pant legs had two big muddy circles on them, and of course my foot was so caked with mud that it looked like I had been living in the woods for weeks.

He continued. "I'm not happy that you and Dasher would do something as dangerous as walking through the woods at night." He paused to turn up the heat. "But between you and me, I'm proud that you faced your fear of germs and got . . . honestly, *filthy*. Unfortunately, you're still going to have to face Mom."

I nodded. She was scarier than Dad when it came to punishments.

But if I had it to do all over again, I'd still go out there and do everything I did—even if it meant being grounded. Part of me wished I could've made it the whole night in the woods. But I was happy to get home—I really had to go to the bathroom.

When I got home, Mom grounded me from cooking for a week, which would be torture since I had an idea for a Black Forest Cake Cookie, inspired by the woods at night. And Dasher texted me that she had to help her mom with dinner for the next two weeks.

Too bad we can't switch parents, I texted her.

It was good to be friends.

The next two weeks flew by as Dasher and I frantically tried to teach each other last-minute skills before the Sleeping Bear race.

"Remember to always check for pieces of eggshell in the batter, and use a powdered-sugar spoon to remove them," I told Dasher.

"Never yell at the dogs—they can hear you just fine if you talk softly."

"Let the batter sit a couple of minutes before you pour it onto the skillet."

"Squat down when you're going through fields to avoid the wind slowing you down."

"Wipe off your spatula between pancakes with a paper towel for both cleanliness and to make it easier to get under the pancakes."

"As you approach the finish line, start pedaling to help the dogs when they're tired."

When our last few weeks were up, we were officially ready.

Chapter 26

"Yum," I said, opening the container of Champion Cheesecake Burritos Lily had brought over. "These look delicious."

"And I wrapped each one individually so you can easily eat them while racing."

I guessed she had forgotten that 1) the race was only four miles; 2) I would never let go of the handlebar to eat because I'd be holding on for dear life; and 3) there wasn't time to eat—it'd be awful to lose by a burrito. But I smiled anyway. They'd be good for the car, at least.

"Thanks," I said. "I know Michigan's far, but I wish you could come watch."

"Me too, but Via and I promised Mrs. Rodriguez that on

Saturday we'd try to get the chocolate from the crocheting party off the ceiling."

Via had to be the worst chef on the planet. Good thing I got paired with Dasher instead of her.

"Well, Mom's waiting outside," Lily said. "Good luck—or do I say break a leg?"

"Definitely don't say that!" I laughed. "And once all of our project stuff is over, maybe we can start cooking again. You, me, *and* Dasher. And Via. Dasher's really gotten . . . well, better at it."

"That's fab. Oh, wait." She reached into her pocket. "Via wanted me to give you this." Lily handed me a bracelet made of glittery letter beads that spelled out GOOD LUCK. Only Via would think to give jewelry to a musher. It was actually really sweet.

"Tell her thanks," I said, slipping it on my wrist.

After saying goodbye to Lily, I put the bag of burritos into the cooler next to my backpack. I looked through the box of baking supplies I'd put together for Dasher one more time. Since she was supplying the dogs, the sled, and all the gear, I was bringing all the specialty ingredients she'd need for the pancakes.

"Got everything?" Mom asked. "We'll be leaving pretty early tomorrow morning."

"I think so." I looked down at my hands. Now that it was coming down to it, I was getting nervous. When that happened, I started to think about germs and needing to wash them off, even though it really didn't help that much.

"You sure you don't want to call Dr. Taylor to talk through anything?" Mom asked, touching my arm.

"I'm positive."

Dr. Taylor would probably tell me to eat dog fur or something.

Friday morning, Mom, Dad, and I left for the race. The six-hour ride to Michigan wasn't so bad. Dasher and I even got to miss school. Mom had rented sled dog movies as well as the first season of my favorite baking competition show. While Dad drove, she sat in the back of the car with me, and we ate popcorn and candy like we were sitting at the movies.

After we settled in at the hotel, I knocked on Dasher's hotel room door to say hello and to drop off the box of baking supplies. I was greeted by my team.

"Hi, Biscuit, hi, Tulip . . . and hi, Gravy!" Gravy had come along as my backup dog. "Where's Dracula?" I asked, looking around. "He's not injured, is he? I haven't practiced much with Gravy." I started panicking. Although Dasher had sometimes had me run Gravy in case Tulip or Dracula couldn't race, I didn't trust him as much.

"No, no. Dracula's fine. He's just not housebroken," Dasher told me. "Most sled dogs aren't."

"Yeah, all of Dad's dogs are naughty and have no manners," Cubby added.

"So where are they staying tonight?" I asked as Biscuit jumped onto the bed and got comfy in the middle.

"In the truck," Cubby answered. "In their dog boxes."

The Hopkinses had a really cool truck with a big wooden box in the back that had little separate sections for the dogs.

"Are you all set for tomorrow, Ana?" Mrs. Hopkins asked.

"I have no idea. Should I be stretching, or praying, or what?"

"I'd say just relax and keep warm while you can," she answered. "It's supposed to be pretty cold in the morning."

"Yeah—a perfect day for racing," Dasher said, rummaging through the box of supplies I had brought. "So, I use a *teaspoon*, not a *tablespoon*, of salt for the chocolate pancakes, right? And the eggs, do I beat them before mixing them in the Hawaiian recipe or once they're in the batter? What if I poison someone—you know, like those fish that need to be cut a certain way because if they're not, they're deadly?"

"Blowfish?" I asked.

"Yeah, blowfish! Do I have any ingredients in here that can be dangerous if I mix them wrong?"

Mrs. Hopkins and I laughed. "I don't think so," I said, although I could've rattled off all the potential dangers of raw eggs and meat from memory. "Your pancakes will be great."

That night, Dasher, Cubby, and I hung out at the hotel's indoor pool. It was fun to forget about everything for a while. That is, until it was bedtime.

We were staying *in a hotel*—a hotel where other people had used the things that I was expected to use. I usually packed my own towels, pillow, and bed sheets, but for this trip, Mom and Dad wouldn't let me. At the time, Mom had managed to convince me I could handle it. Now I wasn't so sure.

"Honey, it's important you remember what Dr. Taylor taught you," Mom said. "Why don't we start by sitting on the bed together and then you can ease your way under the covers?"

"I don't know," I whined. Although part of me knew it was my OCD brain that made me come up with gruesome stories to explain why the bed might be contaminated (a person with the Black Plague slept in it and died a slow death, for instance), I still couldn't get the thoughts out of my head.

"Ana, don't let your OCD tell you what you can and can't do," Dad said, like we were talking about a school bully. "You need a good night's sleep."

Maybe I could stand up all night, or sleep in the car or—

There was a knock on our door, and Mom went to open it. "Hi, Dasher."

"I have a surprise for Ana." She held up her tablet. "Someone wants to say hi."

There, on the other end, was Sweet Pea sitting in her doghouse with her head poking out.

I took the tablet. "Hi, Sweet Pea! I miss you so much!"

She licked her lips.

"I'm doing my first race tomorrow."

She licked her lips again.

"Who are you talking with? Lily?" Dad asked, coming over to the doorway.

"Is that Sweet Pea? She's so precious!" Mom said, peeking over my shoulder.

We sat there as if waiting for her to say something.

"Anyway," Dasher said. "Thanks, Margo." Margo was one of the four dog sitters the Hopkins family needed whenever they went somewhere overnight. "See you tomorrow." She clicked off the tablet.

"Thanks," I said to Dasher.

"And one more surprise . . ." She pulled something out of her back pocket. "Ta-da!" She unfolded a picture of Sweet Pea. It was a little blurry, but she was still adorable.

"Double thanks!" I grinned. I remembered back to when I didn't think anyone would ever get me besides Lily. I had been so wrong.

Once Dasher left, I pulled out a picture of Bernie Toast I had packed in my suitcase, too. I set the two pictures side-by-side on the bed. Bernie looked like he was grinning. I sure missed him. Looking at his picture made me feel like he was still with me.

Dad patted my arm and smiled as he walked past me.

And Sweet Pea . . . through everything, she'd been the best OCD therapy ever. Whenever I felt a little worried, I just squeezed her and it soaked up my bad thoughts like a sponge. Since she couldn't be here, the picture would have to do tonight.

Sweet Pea stared back at me from her photo with her big sad eyes. *Wow, I can't believe I tried to race her*, I thought. I knew so much more about what made a good sled dog than I had even a couple weeks before.

I could do it—I *would* do it. But first I'd need a good night's sleep.

I closed my eyes, took a deep breath, and crawled into the bed. In order to race tomorrow, I'd have to rough it tonight.

"Just look at that," Dad said, holding open the hotel room window's curtain. He sighed. "It snowed."

"And that's bad?" I ran to the window. "Yay! It'll be perfect for racing. I wonder if they needed to break the trail." I pulled out a spare pair of wool socks from the pack Dasher had given me as a gift and tossed them to Mom. "You might need these."

Mom and Dad looked at one another. "What have you done with our daughter?" Dad joked.

He was right. A year before I never would've imagined being excited about snow, or dogs. I didn't even know then that sled dog racing existed.

"You all set?" Mom asked.

I grabbed my coat, hat, and the picture of Sweet Pea. "Yep."

As we drove to the race site, I could feel myself getting more and more nervous. *What if I get lost in the woods? What if it takes me so long to finish that everyone leaves? Or worse, what if everyone sits out in the cold waiting for me to eventually finish, and when I get there, they've all become human ice sculptures?*

"Here we are," Dad said, pulling into the resort. "Now we just have to find Little Bear Hill." We wove around past cabins and a ski area to where the race would be held.

Dad parked the car next to a truck with a huge wooden box in the back. A bunch of dog snouts were poking out through little doors on the front. I smiled and popped open my seatbelt.

"Let's see," Mom said, looking at the schedule she had printed. "You have about twenty minutes before registration opens and your drivers' meeting starts."

"Okay. I'm going to say hi to Dasher at the pancake breakfast," I said. As I opened the car door, the frigid air and the sound of millions of dogs barking and howling rushed in. I took in the noises that had become a melody to me over the weeks of practice.

Wow. There were dogs everywhere. In boxes in pickup trucks. Attached to drop chains on picket lines going from trucks to nearby poles. Some dogs were being walked; others were in kennels. Everywhere you turned: dogs, all waiting for their race to begin.

To my left was a team of all medium-sized blond-and-white ones. *Alaskan Huskies,* I told myself. And to my left was a team of huge black-and-white ones. *Malamutes*. There were teams with Eurohounds like the Hopkinses' dogs, too.

As I headed into the building where the pancake breakfast was, I was hit by the smell of something burning. Uh-oh. I hurried in.

The room had tons of tables set up for people to eat at, although there were only a few families inside right then. I pulled my hair back into a ponytail and went into the kitchen.

"Hi, Dasher!" I said. "How are things going?" I cringed, waiting for her answer.

"Great!" she smiled, her braces sparkling. She had on a crooked chef's hat (my present to her), and her messy brown hair poked out from underneath. "Everyone loves our pancakes!"

"More of the Hawaiians," one of the servers said, grabbing a plate of chocolate pancakes and carrying them out.

"The kids all love the chocolate ones," Dasher explained. "And the adults like the Hawaiians. I decided to have the servers talk up the lavender ones and debut them at noon."

"Great. So . . . what do I smell?" I asked, wondering how many batches she'd burned. "I mean, any problems?"

"Well, at first I had the griddle on too high, but I learned my lesson." She moved closer to me and whispered, "See that lady over there?" I looked at an elderly woman wiping down a countertop. "She wanted to stick to her plain old pancake recipe." Dasher motioned to the untouched stack of pancakes. "I've been busy nonstop making mine."

"Wow, that's awesome!"

"Hey, what are you doing in here, anyway?" Dasher asked, stirring batter in a huge bowl. "Don't you have a meeting?"

I looked up at the clock. "Yeah, I better go. Have fun!"

"I'll have Cubby tell me your bib number so I can come help you out of the chute," Dasher said. She looked at the small pitcher in front of her. "Oh, I need to make more pineapple syrup."

"Okay. See you then!"

After I registered, I went over to the tent for the junior mushers' meeting, where I'd also find out my bib number. There were three divisions of junior races. Twelve other kids were in my three-dog division. They all looked like professional mushers with their fancy racing jackets; three of the kids were even wearing clothes with sled dog company logos on them.

"Welcome, junior mushers!" a woman yelled so we could hear her over all of the barking and howling. "You'll begin over there." She pointed to where the starting chute was. "I'll announce your number so you'll know when to start heading over with your team. Once there, wait for the countdown. Teams will head out every two minutes. The trail is well marked, except in one spot, where trail help is standing by to guide you."

"A-oooo! A-ooo!" a nearby dog howled, and the lady waited until he quieted down.

"If you need to drop a dog, be sure to move off the trail and secure it in your sled bag." She continued going over the race route. "And remember, have fun out there!"

Before we left, we each drew a bib number to know the order we'd be racing in. I walked back to the car with mine.

Mom and Dad were still sitting in the heated car, now cradling cups of coffee in their hands. "I'm number three out of twelve," I said.

"A leader of the pack," Dad said smiling.

I gulped and made A's in my coat pocket. He was right—I'd be near the front.

"I better find my team." I walked around until I found Mr. Hopkins getting his sled set up. He was racing in the adult division later in the day.

"Hey, Ana," he said, looking up. "I was hoping you'd show."

"Too late to back out now, right?" I said, half joking, half not.

"Let me help you get set up."

We walked over to the drop line my dogs were attached to. "You ready, guys?" I asked Tulip, Biscuit, and Dracula. They were jumping up and down.

Mr. Hopkins helped me get all my lines in place in front of the sled.

"Thanks. And thanks for letting me use Dasher's sled. And your dogs."

He pulled off his hat and shoved it in his back pocket. "Trust me—these dogs are thankful that you're running them today. And having someone in Illinois who's into the sport . . . man, it means everything to Dasher."

I knew what that was like—if Lily didn't like baking as much as I did, I don't know what I'd do with myself.

Actually, I did survive without Lily for a while. But not without Dasher.

"There," Mr. Hopkins said, scratching Dracula behind his ears. "You're all set. I've seen you practice—you'll do great."

"Thanks. So will you."

I hopped on the sled and practiced stepping on the brake. After that, there wasn't much I could do except wait for my race to begin.

Mom, Dad, and I went to watch the little kids' one-dog race—*the one I probably should be in*, I thought nervously. It was too bad that Mr. and Mrs. Hopkins wouldn't let Cubby race until next year. I bet he would've won—or, at least, done better than me.

One by one, the kids went off on a short trail, their mom or dad walking the dog to the halfway point, turning them around, and then letting the dogs run to the finish line. One boy was crying before his number was even called. I hoped that wouldn't be me in a little while.

After that race finished and the last musher lined up for the two-dog race, we headed back to the Hopkinses' truck, where Mr. Hopkins helped me clip the dogs onto the gang line.

"Team number three, on deck," the woman yelled into the megaphone.

My stomach dropped.

It was time.

RECIPE FOR RACING

3 sled dogs
3 harnesses
1 gang line
3 tug lines
2 neck lines
1 sled with sled bag
1 snow hook
2 dog handlers
1 worried musher

1. Harness all dogs.
2. Lay out gang line and clip onto the front of the sled. Attach tug lines and neck line to it.
3. Have handlers help to get the dogs attached to the gang line and hold on to them until the countdown.
4. Wait for the word "Go!" and allow handlers to release the dogs.
5. STAY ON THE SLED!

Chapter 27

"I'm here! I'm here!" Dasher shouted, running over as fast as her ankle would let her.

She and Cubby grabbed hold of Tulip's and Dracula's collars to walk them to the starting line so they wouldn't take off early.

"Honey, are you all ready?" Mom asked, as I put my helmet on.

I nodded, even though my knees were shaking hard enough to churn butter.

"You look a little . . . pale. You okay?" Dasher asked. She leaned over to me. "You could still back out, you know. If you need to."

"No. I'm doing this." I stepped onto the sled's runners and pulled up the snow hook. We all headed over to the start line, my dogs pulling me there while I rode the brake.

"Any last questions?" Dasher asked.

Yes—what have I gotten myself into? Instead, I asked, "How many pancakes did you end up making?"

She laughed. "Like, a billion. I may go down in the Guinness World Records for Most Pancakes Made at a Sled Dog Race."

We lined up behind team number two. "Three, two, one. Go!" the timer shouted, and the team in front of me took off like a shot from a cannon. The crowd on the sides of the starting line cheered.

"All right, come on," Mr. Hopkins said to the dogs, and we moved up to the line. "Two minutes, Ana."

"Mr. Hopkins, can you hold the brake a minute?" I asked, and he took my place on the sled.

I walked over to my team. "Okay, Dracula and Tulip. This is it. This is what we've been training for. Just do your best, okay?" I petted them with my gloved hand. "And you, too, Biscuit. You're just as important." Biscuit jumped up and down.

"Thirty seconds," the timer told me as I got back on the sled. I looked over at Mom and Dad, who were standing in front of the crowd. Dad was smiling, and Mom was happy crying. I waved nervously.

"Ten, nine, eight, seven . . ."

Was it too late to back out? I could see if Dasher's ankle was good enough . . .

"Six, five, four . . ."

I breathed in and out. Dasher gave me a thumbs-up. I pictured Bernie Toast smiling down at me, saying, "No worries," Lily telling me to go for it, Sweet Pea licking my feet, and even Via giving me a good-luck bracelet.

"Three, two, one. Go!"

Dasher and Cubby let go of my lead dogs, and I lifted up on the brake. I shouted, "Hike!" although I didn't need to. Dracula and Tulip were already off running.

The crowd cheered as I whizzed past.

I clenched the handlebar. *We can do this.*

"Gee!" I shouted, and the dogs turned right. I leaned into the turn, just like Dasher had shown me so many times.

"Good job!" I squealed. The dogs were doing it—they were racing. And I was leading them—well, I suppose Tulip was leading Dracula and Biscuit, but I was in charge. I was in charge for a sport!

We kept going, weaving along the trail through the snow. I kept my eyes peeled for turns and weird stuff on the trail, but the dogs seemed to know what they were doing already.

I heard a team coming up behind me. We moved over to the side so they could pass. Musher number five. I hoped number four wasn't going to pass us as well.

Just as we were hitting a good pace, the trail turned left, and my team took it flawlessly. Phew. The trail straightened out for the next mile.

I breathed in the cold air. I totally understood why Dasher

liked this so much. Not only being with the dogs, but the excitement of the race—and knowing that there were fans at the end waiting to cheer me on. I definitely wanted to do this again.

"Keep it up!" I said.

But after we had gotten a good groove going, Tulip stopped for a bathroom break. She squatted down, causing Biscuit to crash into her and tangle the line. Then Tulip started running again with Biscuit in front of her.

"Stop, Biscuit!" I said. "Whoa. Everybody stop!" I stepped hard on the brake. They finally halted and looked back at me as if to say, "What are you doing? We're in a race."

But they were a tangled mess.

"Oh no! What do we do?" I asked them. I wasn't anywhere close to the point where there were volunteers waiting to help me. "I can't do this!"

I put my hands over my face. I was in way over my head.

And then I remembered what Grammy had said about taking a recipe step by step.

But first I needed to breathe.

Breathe in, breathe out.

I scooted us off to the side of the trail as well as I could.

Step one: secure the snow hook. I dropped it to the ground while still pressing down on the brake. Then I jammed it into the snow with one foot. As the dogs moved forward, it actually stuck!

I remembered to get off on the other side of the sled and hurried over to the dogs.

Biscuit's line was crossed over Tulip's.

As I tried to figure out the best way to untangle them, a team blew past me, the musher yelling "On by!"

One team closer to finishing last, I thought, but I shook the worry out of my head.

Step two: Concentrate on getting one dog separated at a time.

"Let's see here . . ." I looked at all the lines.

A third team came up behind me. "Need help?" the girl asked, slowing.

"No, I think I'm all right."

"I'll let the checkpoint person know," she said, and continued on.

"Come on, team. We can do this." Another team passed. "But we have to move fast."

Holding Dracula with one hand, I was able to get Biscuit to back up. "Good girl, Biscuit." I moved Tulip one way, and then the other. Then I checked that all my lines were straight. I did it!

Step three: Remove the snow hook.

I pushed down on the brake and bent into what Cubby called the Twister position to grab the snow hook. I leaned back, pulled it out of the ground, and snapped up. "Hike!"

And we were off again—racing along the trail like naturals. I was in the woods by myself, mushing dogs!

It was a beautiful trail, with a maze of trees that looked like tall pretzel rods poking out of the ground, parts of them white-chocolate covered.

The cold air didn't feel offensive—it felt . . . natural. Fresh. Piney.

As I approached the next corner, the checkpoint person shouted, "Almost done. Keep it up!"

The race course was basically a large U-shape with a ton of little twists and turns. It ended pretty much back where it started, so the spectators got to see both the start and end of the race.

"Haw!" I shouted, and we turned left. The finish line was in sight. "Okay, guys, time to pick it up!"

The dogs tried to go faster, but I could tell they were tired. There were two teams in sight in front of me. They, too, didn't seem to be going as fast as they had been before.

I remembered when Dad used to run in the Fourth of July 5K race. He said he always made it his goal to at least beat the person right in front of him.

As my dogs slowed, I began pedaling to help them out. "Pick it up, pick it up!"

I pushed and pushed the ground with my foot. We got closer to team six. "We can do it. Hup, hup!"

Finally my team pulled in front of them. "Keep it up!" I said as we stayed ahead. *I actually passed a team!*

"Come on, Team Morgan!" Cubby shouted from just past the finish line.

Since I was getting tired, I put my foot back on the runner and stayed low like Dasher had taught me. And just in time. The dogs got one last surge of energy and whizzed through the finish line.

"Whoa!" I shouted as we passed the timer. Cubby and Dasher grabbed the dogs' collars as they slowed.

I did it. I did it! My lungs had no air left in them, but I'd done it!

"Oh, honey! You were great!" Mom said, coming over to hug me.

"Wahoo! You did awesome!" Dasher said, putting her hand out for a high five. "And the finish—you guys came in strong!"

"I . . . had . . . a . . . great . . . teacher," I said between breaths.

"It's not the teacher but the driver who's key," Dasher said.

"And the dogs," we both said.

"Here, let me take your team back so you can catch your breath," Mr. Hopkins said, giving me a chance to hop off. "Great run, Ana. Really great." He steered the sled back to the truck while Cubby and Dasher kept hold of Tulip's and Dracula's collars.

I took off my helmet and rubbed down my sweaty hair.

"You're a natural!" Dad said, patting my back.

"I'm so proud of you!" Mom said, tears in her eyes again.

"That was the best thing ever!" I squealed. "The dogs couldn't have done better! Omigod—I didn't tell them how good they did! Be right back!"

I ran to catch up with my team.

Dasher and Cubby were hooking the dogs onto the drop chains so they could have water.

I ran over to Tulip first. "Good girl!" I gave her a big hug, and she licked my face. "You ran great! And you, too, Dracula! What a pair you two made. And, Biscuit, you did a super job as wheel." I rubbed behind her ears.

"So what'd you think?" Dasher asked.

"It was the coolest thing I've ever done. They turned corners like pros, moved over for other teams . . ."

"Any problems?"

I had almost forgotten! "Eh, a little snag for a minute, but we worked it out."

"I'm so jealous! I can't wait to get back on a sled," she said. "Oh, shoot—I need to get back to the pancake breakfast. Hey, you wanna help now that you're done? People liked our pancakes so much, they said they'd be back later with friends. We're going to be swamped!"

I looked over at the dogs. "In a little bit. I'm going to get their food and then watch the start of the next race."

"You—choosing mushing over cooking?"

I smiled. "What can I say—I was born to mush."

Later that day, the officials posted the results for all the races. Mr. Hopkins got first for his division and won a huge trophy and a bunch of money, which he said he'd use to take us all out for pizza back home.

I finished tenth in the three-dog division.

I didn't expect to win, or even get fifth or anything. It wouldn't even have mattered if I had come in last—but I was pretty pleased that I hadn't.

Chapter 28

On the way home from the race, we stopped by Grammy's, which was only a half hour out of the way. After scrounging around in her cabinets, she and I whipped up a dessert. "Ana did just wonderfully today," Mom said while we ate. "I wish you could have come, Mrs. Crawford."

"My knees don't like the cold so much," Grammy said. "But you enjoyed your first race?"

I swallowed a spoonful of whipped topping. "Yeah! I never thought I'd like sled dog racing."

"It doesn't surprise me," Grammy said, wiping her mouth with a cloth napkin and setting it back on her lap. "You've always loved animals, haven't you?"

I nodded.

"*And* you're a risk taker," she added.

"Me?" I scrunched up my nose.

"Absolutely. You've faced your own fears without even realizing it."

Mom and Dad nodded, too.

"You mean my OCD?" I asked and shook my head. "My therapist forced me to do my ERP—I didn't want to."

"I wasn't talking about that OCDC thing. I was talking about all this sled dogging stuff. *You* are responsible for facing your thoughts."

"I had to do it—Dasher hurt her ankle, and I had to mush in her place."

Grammy spooned up a banana chunk. "No, you could have put together a bake sale for the race, or helped Dasher's dad train. You didn't have to race. And if you can train yourself for a sport where dogs are the main equipment, I think you can do anything."

I smiled. After all I had gone through the past few months with Dasher and Lily and Bernie and Sweet Pea, part of me actually believed her.

We drove home Saturday night, arriving after midnight.

Sunday afternoon, Dad drove me over to the Hopkinses'. I had made a special treat for Dracula, Tulip, and Biscuit:

Doggie's Delicious Casserole, made with leftover chicken, carrots, and peas. Of course, I had made a little extra for Sweet Pea as well.

"Bye," I said to Dad when we arrived, but he began getting out of the car, too.

"I need to talk to Mr. Hopkins for a minute," he said. I shrugged and met Dasher at the door.

"How do you feel?" Dasher asked as we walked to the kitchen. It smelled like cookies.

"A little stiff—I think from clenching the handlebar during the race." I set down my casserole.

"It's intense, huh?"

"The last time my hands hurt this bad was when I whipped egg whites by hand for a meringue. Speaking of: are you actually *baking? For fun?*"

"I kinda like it now." She opened the oven and peeked at her cookies. "Are they done?"

I looked over her shoulder. "No, they still look raw in the center."

She closed the oven door. "Wouldn't it be so awesome if we both raced next year? We'd just expand on our project from this year." Dasher smiled but then smacked her forehead. "Duh. You probably want to do a cooking project with Lily. Well, anyway."

"I don't know. Mushing was a pretty cool topic. But we have a whole year to think about it. And, regardless, we can still race for fun."

"Yeah," she said, grabbing a potholder that looked like a dog opening its mouth. "And if we end up in Mr. Creed's English class again, who knows who we'll be partnered with."

"There's always Ben and his stamp collection," I said, and we both laughed. "Oh, I almost forgot. I brought a treat for my team. Can I take it out to them?"

"Sure."

First I delivered Dracula his treat, which he lapped right up. Then I went over to the girls' pen. Biscuit and Tulip jumped on top of their doghouses, their tails wagging. "Well, you're either happy to see me, or you smell my casserole," I said, opening the gate and going in. I spooned it into their food bowls, saving some for Sweet Pea. "I'll be right back."

But when I walked over to her doghouse, it was empty. I looked around the pen, the hairs on the back of my neck prickling. "Sweet Pea?" She wasn't in the yard.

I ran back into the house. "Sweet Pea . . ." I started, out of breath. "She isn't in the dog yard. Is she in the house?"

Dasher smooshed a cookie while trying to get it off the cookie sheet. "No . . ."

I gasped. "She escaped! When did you last see her? Do you think she went to the same spot in the woods as last time? I know exactly where to look."

"I think my dad took her for a walk or something," she said, not even looking up at me.

"Really? Why would your dad take Sweet Pea for a walk? Doesn't he have, like, twenty of his own dogs to care for?"

"No, I forgot. Cubby took her to the park to play catch."

"Cubby with Sweet Pea?" That was a first.

"I think he felt bad about having her mush."

I relaxed.

"We better start thinking about the backboard for our project," Dasher said. "My mom took some really good pictures of you at the race, and of my pancakes."

"And we have the write-up to do, too," I added.

She groaned. "You wanna go outside and help with the dogs while my cookies cool?"

"No, what if we just work on the backboard today and do the write-ups on our own?" I said and then snapped my fingers. "What if you write about the first half of the mushing stuff and the second half of the baking stuff, and I'll do the opposite."

"It'll be like I turned into you and you turned into me."

We smiled at each other. It wasn't so far off.

Once we finished working on our backboard, Mr. Hopkins dropped me off at home.

"I'm home!" I yelled.

"We're in the kitchen," Mom called back.

As I set down my backpack, I heard the familiar jingling of a dog collar coming toward me. But we didn't have a dog.

Sweet Pea jingled over with a big grin on her face. She sat

down in front of me and looked up at me with her sweet chocolate eyes.

"Huh? Sweet Pea? What are you doing here?" I put out my hand for her to lick. "Hi, girl."

Sweet Pea and I walked into the kitchen, where Mom and Dad were getting ready for dinner. By the laundry room door was a large bag of dog food, a bowl of water, and a food dish that read I ♥ THE CHEF.

"You have quite the dog there, Ana," Dad said, pouring himself some water. "You're going to make a wonderful dog owner."

"Wh-what do you mean?"

Mom and Dad looked at one another and smiled.

"We know how much you miss Bernie, and what good care you've taken of Sweet Pea," Dad said. "I asked Mr. Hopkins if he'd be willing to let us adopt her." He patted Sweet Pea's back. "She's all yours."

"No way! Did you hear that, Sweet Pea? You're a Morgan!" She wagged her tail. I wasn't sure which of us was happier.

When I went to my room, I found a pink dog bed next to my own bed. Sweet Pea sauntered over to it and lay down like she'd been living there her whole life. I thought of Bernie and how he would have loved her.

Just as I was about to text her, Dasher called.

"Omigod! I can*not* believe I have a dog!" I blubbered. "Did you know?"

"Your dad called and asked about adopting her." She

laughed. "It was so hard not to say anything when you came over."

"And you're okay giving her up?" I asked.

"Are you kidding? I've never seen either of you happier than when you're together. Sweet Pea's more of a house dog anyway. And she can always come over and visit the other dogs with you."

Just then Lily texted.

"Hold on a minute," I told Dasher as I read the message.

I need help with our catering business. Via and I are really in a bind.

I have a surprise! I texted. You have to come over. Via too.

"Hey, you wanna come over?" I asked Dasher. "We have an Explorations emergency."

Chapter 29

"Hey," Lily said, letting herself in.

Before I even got a chance to tell Lily about Sweet Pea, the two of them met at the door.

"A dog! No way! That is so fab!" Lily squealed.

"This is Sweet Pea," I told her.

"Nice to meet you, Sweet Pea. Ana is the best pet mother ever. Hey, now you have someone to clean up the floors when you cook."

I laughed, and my new dog lay down at my feet.

"So what's your problem?" I asked Lily.

The bell rang.

"Long time, no see," Dasher said walking in.

Lily explained how she and Via had catered a film group on Saturday, and Via had been in charge of the cupcakes.

"I figured—easy peasy," Lily said. "She'd just make a box of cake mix. What could go wrong? Well, the cupcakes *looked* fine. But when the guests bit into them, they all made horrible faces. It turns out she forgot to buy frosting and just added sugar to the jar of mayo that was in her pantry. Talk about something belonging in our Disasters section."

"Yuck," Dasher said.

"Exactly," Lily said. "Some of the guests weren't so nice about it," Lily said. "They said we shouldn't be in business if we didn't know how to bake. *I* know how to bake."

"Of course you do." I rubbed Sweet Pea behind the ears. "So you guys had one bad catering job. There are plenty of other groups out there."

"That was our fourth bad gig." Lily began petting Sweet Pea, too. "I mean, I love Via to death, but I asked her to make a piece of toast for a dish I was trying, and she even burned that. At this point, we just need simple things that taste good to get business again. You'd think that wouldn't be so hard."

I looked at Dasher. "Any ideas?"

"Maybe, but let's wait for Via."

That's when the bell rang again. "OMG," Via squealed when she met Sweet Pea. "She's ridiculously adorable! Does she race?"

"No!" Dasher and I said at the same time and burst out laughing.

"Okay, ladies," Lily said. "Back to the problem. How can we get more business?"

"Maybe," Dasher started, "you could give away samples of your food with a flyer that has your business logo on it. Like at a bake sale or something."

"But where would we do a bake sale?" Via asked.

"A basketball game?" Dasher suggested.

"But you can't make money at a basketball game. The school wouldn't let you." I tapped my lip. "Unless . . . the money could go to charity. Maybe an animal shelter?"

Lily and Via looked at each other and nodded.

"And we could help with the bake sale!" I said.

"Definitely," Dasher added. "If you want my help, that is."

"She's really good at pancakes," I added.

"Oh, oh, I know," Dasher said. "Since it's for an animal shelter, you could have dog treats, too."

"Perfect!" Lily said. "So you guys will help make the food? Please, please, please!"

We worked for two hours, each of us making our own mixture for the dog treats. The kitchen was a mess with various meat broths, dog foods, frozen vegetables, canned pumpkin, and peanut butter.

Occasionally, I'd look around and think, *Did anyone touch a spoon with their finger and then reuse it?* or *Is Via breathing too close to the mixture?* but each time I took a deep breath and reminded myself that if my family could eat cookies I dipped my finger in, dogs could eat treats made with a spoon that was used more than once.

"So how do we know which recipe to use?" Via asked.

"That's easy," I said and bent down. "Sweet Pea? You want a treat?" Her ears perked up.

We each set a small piece of our biscuit in front of her and waited. One by one, she sniffed them, then snarfed each up. We laid out a second set of each. This time she went right for Via's.

"And I think we have a winner!" Lily announced.

"Really?" Via said. "And I didn't think I was even good at cooking."

"It's ironic how this has gone full circle," Mom said as she drove me to the basketball game. "Isn't this just what you wanted your Explorations project to be?"

It wasn't exactly how I had planned it, but it was pretty close.

Once we got to the gym, Lily, Via, and I set up a table near the Student Council's popcorn machine. Lily also made a sign that read SUPPORT FAIRY TAILS ANIMAL RESCUE—BUY OUR TREATS. NOT ONLY WILL YOU LOVE THEM, BUT SO WILL YOUR DOG.

As we were laying out our treats, Dasher showed up.

"Sorry I'm late. But I had copies of flyers made at my dad's office." She sheepishly laid down a stack of flyers with drawings of a muffin and teacup. The steam from the tea spelled out the words CLASSEE CATERING COMPANY in fancy cursive. "I tried making a logo for your company . . . You don't have to use them though."

"You are, like, the coolest," Via told her. "I wish I could draw!"

"I can teach you," Dasher said with a smile.

And it turned out our fundraiser was a hit. Our Everything Cookies sold out in forty-five minutes, and people thought the dog treats were such an original idea. Luckily, Via and Lily had made enough for the entire city.

As things were winding down, we saw Mr. Creed crossing the gym.

"Good evening, Ms. Hopkins. Ms. Morgan. Ms. Kirkland."

"Good evening, Mr. Creed," we all answered. I made A's on the floor with my shoe.

"What are we vending this evening?" He squinted to read our flyer. I quickly skimmed it for typos and contractions.

"W-we have cereal pies and coconut-orange cupcakes," Dasher stammered. "We sold out of our Everything Cookies, sir."

"Everything Cookies?" he questioned.

"They are a combination of three different cookies," Dasher said. "Sir."

"Not exactly a treat for the palate." He picked up a bag of dog treats. "And what is this concoction?" He smelled the bag and made a face.

"Those are dog treats," Via said, smiling. "I came up with the recipe."

"Dog treats? At a basketball game?" And Mr. Creed did something I'd never seen before. He smiled. "Although it is not a conventional venue for dog treats, I do like that it is an original idea. How much is a bag?"

"Two dollars," Lily answered.

"I will take five bags."

"What kinda dog do you have?" Via asked him.

Mr. Creed handed over the ten dollars and also pulled out his phone. "This is Princess, my Chihuahua." Princess was dressed in a pink tutu and had matching bows on her ears.

"Cute!" we all squealed.

"So this is part of your Explorations project, I imagine," he said to Dasher, Via, and me.

"Yes, sir," Dasher said. "We decided to combine our skills."

"I look forward to seeing how it turns out," he said. And he left.

"Wow, that was scary," Lily said. "But I guess he isn't such a bad guy after all."

"I wonder if he's ever considered racing Princess," Dasher

said. Via, Lily, and I gave her a funny look, and she shrugged. "Any dog can pull, you know."

By the time Explorations Day rolled around, Dasher and I were all set. We had decided to make one side of our display board all about the race itself—the work with the sled dogs and my training. The other was all about cooking—Dasher learning to cook, the pancake breakfast, and the fundraiser we helped Lily and Via with. We decorated the border of the board with dog prints, and Dasher drew a huge picture of a sled dog eating a tall stack of pancakes with a fork and knife.

We stood in front of our display wearing matching ski hats and Sleeping Bear Sled Dog Race sweatshirts that Mr. Hopkins had bought us with some of his prize money. We also had samples of our chocolate pancakes.

The judges would start walking around soon, and other classes were starting to filter in.

"We still have to decide what to say," Dasher said.

"You didn't write up anything?" I asked, although I wasn't that surprised.

"Nuh-uh. You know what *you're* gonna say?"

At first I had planned on only talking about teaching Dasher how to cook. But then I realized that our project was about more than just the race and the cooking. It was about how I used to be afraid of dogs and dog germs. How Sweet Pea and sled dog training helped me relax a little bit.

How I always thought all I ever wanted to do was cook, but now I kind of wanted to be a veterinarian or run in another sled dog race. And that I had believed I only had room for one friend in my life. But it turns out that friends are like recipes: you can never have too many. And it's always good to try out new ones— no matter how different they seem.

VIA, LILY, ANA, AND DASHER'S DOGGIE DELIGHTS

½ cup whole-wheat flour
¼ cup old-fashioned oats
¼ cup pumpkin puree
1 tbsp water

1. ~~Sanitize baking surface.~~ Preheat oven to 350° F. Cover a baking sheet with parchment paper.
2. Mix flour and oats in a medium-sized bowl.
3. Add in pumpkin puree (you can use your finger to get it off the spoon) and water. Stir together until well mixed.
4. Using 1 tbsp of the dough at a time, shape into balls with your hands (dogs don't mind!). Place on a baking sheet. Press down into a circle with the palm of your hand.
5. Bake for 40 minutes or until hard. Let cool.
6. Feed to your dog.
7. Store in the fridge or freezer.

Original recipe by Via Kirkland
Write-up by Ana Morgan
Idea for dog biscuits by Dasher Hopkins
Sales mainly done by Lily Crawford
Tastings done by Sweet Pea Hopkins-Morgan

Note: Check with your parents before making and feeding to your dog.

Author's Note

Obsessive-compulsive disorder (OCD) is a mental health disorder affecting people of all ages. Although Ana is a fictional character, her symptoms are based on common characteristics of people who are affected by OCD.

OCD causes someone to have unwanted thoughts about something or some things, such as germs, bad things happening, or objects not being in the proper place ("obsessions"). These obsessions give the person a lot of negative feelings, such as fear, guilt, shame, or disgust. They then try to remedy the situation and get rid of these bad feelings by performing behaviors or rituals, such as extreme washing, checking that objects are turned off, or arranging objects a certain way ("compulsions").

These obsessions and compulsions often take up a big part of the person's day, and keep them from being able to live the life they want at home, at school, or with their friends.

OCD can be diagnosed by a mental health professional, such as a psychologist, counselor, or social worker. There are many treatments that can help people with OCD, but the most common treatment shown in this book is Exposure with Response Prevention (ERP), a type of Cognitive Behavioral Therapy (CBT).

In ERP, the person is asked to face what is troubling them—their obsessions—without then using their compulsion(s) to help them get through it. In doing this, they will learn that they can allow the obsessions and bad feelings to come and go without the need for their compulsions to make them disappear.

People are helped and guided through their ERP by a mental health professional. Usually, the person and their therapist will work together to set a "hierarchy," or a group of things their OCD makes them afraid of doing ranked in order of less scary to most scary. The therapist and the person with OCD will then work through these scary things, starting with the less scary and working up to the more scary.

In the case of Ana, her hierarchy started with Dr. Taylor having her first write a script about the worst-case scenario if she stuck her finger in raw cookie-dough batter. Each time she read it, she was bothered by the words and situation less and less. Ana then worked up to actually sticking her finger in the batter and then serving the cookies to her loved ones, which was closer to the top of her hierarchy (in other words, scarier) than writing and reading the script.

If you would like to learn more about OCD, talk to your parents or the school nurse or visit the International OCD Foundation's website at www.OCDinKids.org.

Acknowledgments

There are so many individuals to thank for this book, which began as a grain of salt and became a golden batch of Sprinkle-Cake Cookies.

First, I need to thank the 2008 SCBWI Work-in-Progress committee for choosing my book for a Work-in-Progress grant. This manuscript had been indefinitely stuffed in a drawer. Winning the grant motivated me to keep going.

Next, I need to thank my dog—yes, my dog, Luna, who's the real Sweet Pea. Because she was a puppy and was potty training, she needed to be confined to a small space. The two of us spent our days together in one room until she was trained—and, eventually, I had finished my first draft as well. She has been my office-mate/four-legged cheerleader ever since. Thanks, Luna.

I must thank all of my critique groups who read through endless drafts, including the Dundee and Geneva SCBWI network groups, Sarah and Trina for meet-ups at Panera, and my online KIDSCRIT group.

Then, of course, I have my experts. A big thank-you to Mandy Collins, who, I discovered, is a real-life Dasher. She answered endless Midwest sprint sled dog racing questions for me. To Iditarod musher Pat Moon, who not only answered my early questions, but convinced me to make the journey to Alaska to watch the start of the Iditarod—thanks so much. Thank you to Stephanie Cogen, MPH, MSW, Education and Training Manager for the International OCD Foundation for verifying my obsessive-compulsive disorder facts.

Thanks to those who made this book beautiful, inside and out, starting with Simini Blocker, who did the cover art. Thanks to the team at Sky Pony who made Ana come to life: Ming Liu, Joshua Barnaby, Sammy Yuen, Jenn Chan, Sarah Dean, Kylie Brien, Emma Dubin, Amy Singh, and especially my editor, Rachel Stark, who loved Ana and Sweet Pea as much as I did.

And last but not least, thank you to my family. First to my mom for answering all my grammar-related questions, as well as playing "Kitty" with my kids so I could get work done. To my husband for trusting me to pursue this long journey called writing enough to finally reach the finish line . . . at least with this book. And of course, I must mention my kids, who put up with all our treks to sled dog races, tested out various recipes and actions in my novel, and respected my writing time.

You each deserve a Sprinkle-Cake Cookie!

Natalie Rompella

is the author of more than forty books and educational guides for young readers, and the winner of a Work-in-Progress grant from the Society for Children's Book Writers and Illustrators for an early version of *Cookie Cutters & Sled Runners*. Just like Ana, Natalie grew up baking and inventing her own recipes, and as an adult she fell in love with sled dog racing—watching it, that is! A former museum educator and elementary and middle school teacher, Natalie lives with her family in the Chicago suburbs.